SECRETS

E. A. Briginshaw

E. A. Bri
APRIL 26 2024

ISBN: 978-1-7780648-6-9 (Book)
ISBN: 978-1-7780648-5-2 (eBook)

ACKNOWLEDGMENTS

Although the novel is a work of fiction, some of the characters are composite characters based on my family and friends. Thanks to all of the people who reviewed and critiqued numerous drafts of this novel including friends, members of my family and writers from the Shuswap area of British Columbia.

Table of Contents

Chapter 1..1
Chapter 2 3
Chapter 3 6
Chapter 4 14
Chapter 5 18
Chapter 6 24
Chapter 7 28
Chapter 8 31
Chapter 9 33
Chapter 10...37
Chapter 11 39
Chapter 12..47
Chapter 13..50
Chapter 14..53
Chapter 15..56
Chapter 16..58
Chapter 17..61
Chapter 18..64
Chapter 19..66
Chapter 20 69
Chapter 21..73
Chapter 22 79
Chapter 23 84
Chapter 24 87
Chapter 25 92
Chapter 26 98
Chapter 27 103

CHAPTER 1

"Paging Air Canada passenger, Andrew McKenzie – Air Canada passenger, Andrew McKenzie – please report to the agent at the gate for an important message."

"I'm Andrew McKenzie," I said as I approached the attractive young woman behind the desk.

She smiled. "Are you the journalist who wrote the book about the airline tragedy in Newfoundland?"

Although I was pleased that the book had sold well, I didn't like the notoriety that came with it. "That would be me," I said.

"I *loved* your book," she gushed. "That must have been so scary for you. I mean, my God, every other passenger onboard that plane *died.*"

"Yes, it was quite scary at the time, but here I am, alive and well."

I could see the message in her hand that she was supposed to give me, but it was impossible to read upside-down.

"And that poor woman," she continued, "what was her name?"

"Sarah Khan," I answered.

She kept talking without taking a breath. "What her husband and the police put her through. I probably would have committed suicide if I was in her shoes as well. It was *so* tragic and sad."

"Yes, it was," I said. I could tell she was going to continue talking about the book, so I cut her off before she could get started again. "You said you had an important message for me?"

"Oh yes, sorry." She looked at the paper in her hand. "The message is from Mary Byrnes. Her connecting flight is running late but she said she thinks she'll make it in time for your flight to Qatar. If not, just go on without her and she'll catch the next flight."

Mary was the ICU nurse who had helped me recover after that ill-fated flight in Newfoundland, but she was much more important to me now. We had become lovers, but even that didn't fully describe our relationship. She was my guiding light. She had the ability to cut out all of the extra noise surrounding a person and get them to be the best version of themselves. I don't know how I got so lucky to cross paths with her, and I was determined to live up to her expectations.

Except that I knew there was one secret that I was keeping, not only from her, but from the rest of the world. I had built a reputation as a journalist who dug out the truth and reported on it, no matter how deeply it was buried. But I was a fraud.

I would soon find out that I was not the only one.

CHAPTER 2

As I made my way down the aisle of the aircraft, I could see that someone was already sitting in my seat. Ironically, I had been assigned seat 14C, the same seat as on that disastrous flight almost a year ago. At first I thought that Mary had somehow managed to get onboard the plane before me, but it turned out to be a woman who had mistakenly sat in the wrong seat. She apologized and moved one row back, and I quickly got settled.

Mary came racing through the doors of the aircraft about ten minutes before we were scheduled to depart.

"Boy, that was close," she said as she gave me a hug. "I didn't think I was going to get here in time." She slid into the window seat beside me. "I sure hope my luggage makes it."

Mary had flown into Toronto from Halifax after spending a few days visiting her daughter, who was attending Dalhousie University. This was a work trip for me and I hadn't asked Mary to go with me, but she had insisted.

"Someone's got to be there with you to watch your

back," she'd said. She was extremely nervous about me travelling back to Qatar and Saudi Arabia.

After the plane took off, we were served a meal and watched a movie. Then Mary said she was going to try to get some sleep, but I pulled out my laptop to review my notes and our schedule of meetings over the next few days.

I had digitized all of the papers that Sarah Khan had given me before she'd been arrested. It had taken me a long time to piece together all of the evidence Sarah had gathered, documenting the corruption surrounding the World Cup held in Qatar. The purpose of this trip was to confirm my suspicions and confront some of the individuals involved. It was that last part that had made Mary insist on coming with me.

Mary was familiar with the case because she had acted as my sounding board when I wrote the book about what had happened on board Flight 059. She was aware of how dangerous some of these people were.

The book had been classified as *Fiction – based on a true story*. The publisher, or more accurately, the publisher's lawyers, had insisted we change some of the names and I had agreed. But I wanted the complete story to come out after I confirmed the evidence that Sarah had given me. It would not be easy.

As I reviewed my notes on my laptop, I looked over at Mary who was now sleeping soundly. She was determined to get justice for Sarah Khan, the woman who everyone thought had committed suicide after intense questioning by the police about what had happened on board that flight.

Except Mary didn't know what I knew and I hated not being able to tell her. Sarah Khan was alive and had been placed by RCMP Superintendent Simon Powell in their

Witness Protection Program. Powell had become the fall guy for apparently allowing Sarah to commit suicide under his watch. I had played my part by crucifying him in the media and forcing him to resign.

There were only three people who knew Sarah was still alive: Sarah, Superintendent Powell and myself.

I recalled that Ben Franklin had historically said that the only way three people could keep a secret was if two of them were dead, and I felt a sudden shiver travel down my spine.

CHAPTER 3

After reviewing my notes, I closed my laptop to get some sleep. It was an extremely long flight and I woke up when the cabin crew started their next service. Mary was already awake.

"Did you sleep well?" she asked.

"Not too bad," I said. I was glad that I had upgraded our seats to Premium Economy so we could stretch out a little bit. "How about you?"

"I slept for a few hours," she said, "but I'm starting to get excited. I've never been to this part of the world before." She pointed to the flight tracker display in front of me. "It says we should be landing in Dubai in about three hours."

"It's still a long way to go," I said. "Don't forget that we've got a layover in Dubai of a few hours before our connecting flight to Qatar."

"So what's the plan when we get there?" Mary asked.

"We'll take the first day just to get settled, get our bearings and get used to the time change. Our first scheduled meeting is the day after that with Hassan Al-Thawadi. He headed up the organizing committee for the

Qatar World Cup. The next day I've scheduled an interview with the General Secretary of the Qatar Football Association to get FIFA's perspective, followed by a meeting with one of the main construction contractors for the stadiums. Then we're off to Saudi Arabia to meet with Dawood Khan and his brother, Ahmad."

"*That's* the meeting I'm most nervous about," Mary said.

Me too, I thought to myself. I had interviewed Dawood in Qatar before the World Cup and he had come across as honest, personable and forthcoming. I had believed everything he'd said. Now that his wife Sarah had told me all that he and his brother were capable of, I would not be fooled again.

When we finally made it to Qatar, we discovered that Mary's luggage had failed to make the connecting flight. The airline assured us her luggage would arrive the next day. Fortunately, Mary had packed all of her essentials and one change of clothes in her carry-on bag.

* * *

Despite their assurances, Mary's luggage still hadn't arrived the next day so we headed out to pick up some new clothes for her prior to our first meeting. The dress code in Qatar was not as strict as in other Middle-Eastern countries and non-Qatari women were no longer required to wear the long black robes that we'd seen on TV, nor cover their hair while in public. The clerk at our hotel recommended a shop nearby and Mary had acquired some relatively conservative, but still quite attractive outfits. The key was to wear something below the knees and to always cover your shoulders. Having a shawl proved to be a wise choice, because they always seem to have the air conditioning systems cranked to the limit.

When we arrived at the Supreme Committee's offices, which most people referred to as just the *SC*, we were advised that Hassan Al-Thawadi had been unexpectedly called away and would not be able to meet with us. That was disappointing and I suggested that I hoped we could find a time within the next few days that would work for both of us. We were told that would not be possible.

"The Secretary General has given us full authority to answer your questions on his behalf," the middle-aged man said as he led us into a meeting room that had an impressive view of the city. This man spoke English flawlessly and I had no doubt that he was well educated and spoke several more languages.

He handed me his business card and I noted that he was a lawyer, had a title that was two lines long, and that his first name was Jassim. A woman named Fatima was also in attendance, although it wasn't clear what her role was.

I introduced Mary as my associate and told them we would both be taking notes during the meeting. I started off by congratulating them on holding a very successful World Cup in 2022.

"Yes, we were quite pleased with the event," Jassim said. "Gianni Infantino, the president of FIFA, and a number of other prominent figures in sports, declared the tournament to be the finest ever, owing to the game's inclusion and diversity. We are pleased that the first ever World Cup hosted by a Muslim country, not only for Qatar, but for all of the Middle Eastern countries, proved to be a success."

"Unfortunately," I said, "I'm here investigating various reports of corruption surrounding the awarding and delivery of the event."

Jassim remained stone-faced. "Such as…"

"Let's start off by accusations that members of the FIFA Executive Committee were bribed, not only in awarding the 2022 World Cup to Qatar, but also in awarding the 2018 event to Russia."

"I cannot speak about Russia's World Cup," Jassim said, "but I can assure you that we did not bribe anyone to win the 2022 World Cup. FIFA's two-year internal investigation verified that fact."

"Yes, but the person who headed that study refused to sign off on the report, and the U.S. Justice Department ended up charging fourteen members of the FIFA Executive Council, the council that decides who gets awarded the World Cup events, with various charges of corruption."

"We are aware of those charges," Jassim said, "but most of them relate to individuals stealing money from their own football development league funds. I can assure you that no one was bribed to award the World Cup to Qatar."

"But surely you must agree," I said, "that back in 2010, when both the 2018 and 2022 World Cups were awarded, that the bids from both England and the U.S. were stronger than yours."

"Once again," Jassim said, "I can't comment on the event held in Russia. Qatar did not bid on that World Cup. We only bid on the 2022 event and we were up against South Korea, Japan, Australia and the United States. We submitted a comprehensive proposal and we won – fair and square."

"But there were a lot of risks in awarding you the event," I countered. "Your country is extremely small, you had no stadiums, not enough hotel rooms to accommodate the thousands of people who would be coming to the event, your own team was weak, your country has some questionable human rights policies, and the place is just too darn hot to be playing soccer – sorry – I mean football."

Jassim just smiled. "Yet, despite all of those perceived weaknesses, we just delivered the most successful World Cup ever held."

He had me. The man could counter-punch with the best of them.

"We turned some of those perceived weaknesses into strengths," he continued. "Because we are such a small country, fans could attend more than one match a day and easily move from one stadium to the other. We built all of the stadiums and hotels in time, enough to accommodate 1.4 million guests and 20,000 volunteers. We made sure everyone was safe by deploying…", he looked to Fatima for the numbers.

"32,000 government and 17,000 private security personnel," she interjected.

"All while still allowing the fans to celebrate their wins responsibly," he continued. "The World Cup is an opportunity to bring people together and break down the stereotypes of a lot of different cultures."

"Do you think the ban on selling alcohol during the games helped keep things under control?" I asked.

"Absolutely," Jassim said. "We were initially criticized for that, but I think people realized that you can still enjoy a great football match without using alcohol to fuel the excitement. And there were definitely a lot of great matches, some major upsets along the way, but the final between Argentina and France was classic."

"Yes, I think the whole world celebrated Messi's win," I said. "I guess the only perceived weakness that you didn't solve was the heat issue."

"We actually *had* developed technology to help solve that problem as well," Jassim said. "We had solar-powered systems that cooled the outside air and delivered it through grills in the stands and large nozzles surrounding the pitch. That would have ensured that the fans and players would not have been overcome by the heat."

"Then why did FIFA delay the World Cup until the winter months?" I asked.

"That was their decision," Jassim said. "I think they were nervous that even though we were confident in our new technology, it was unproven and too much of a risk."

I felt myself being swept up in Jassim's enthusiasm about the success of the World Cup and felt a bit guilty about my next question.

"There were also numerous allegations about the abuse of migrant workers during the construction phase of the World Cup sites," I said. "The Indian and Nepalese governments estimated that more than a thousand workers died while working on World Cup projects in Qatar and there were thousands more from other countries."

"We strongly dispute those numbers," Jassim said. "We believe they're including all deaths, even those who died from other causes, and the deaths of people who were not working on our projects. According to *our* records, there were three work-related deaths on World Cup sites and a further 37 non-work-related deaths."

"That's quite a discrepancy in numbers," I said.

"I agree," Jassim said. "But our records have been audited by FIFA and several external agencies, including international unions. We've already documented numerous errors in the numbers they've reported."

"There were also reports of abuse of foreign workers,"

I countered.

"You're referring to the Equidem report," Jassim said.

"Yes, in their report, they indicated that there were numerous instances of worker abuse, wage theft, forced overtime work, and illegal recruitment fees. If the workers complained, they were fired and sent home."

"We did, *initially,* have problems with some of our contractors," Jassim admitted. "In 2016, twenty-five percent of our contractors failed our audits and we stopped using them. We started insisting that all workers be paid electronically so we could verify that they actually received what they were owed. In addition, since FIFA guidelines specified that recruitment fees were illegal, we reimbursed the workers for any of those fees they were forced to pay."

"But according to Qatari law, aren't these workers restricted to only work for the contractor who brought them into the country, even if they're one of your so-called *bad* contractors?"

"With the introduction of our historic labor law reforms, that is no longer the case," Jassim said. "In fact, the UN's International Labor Organization reported that over 240,000 workers were able to switch jobs in Qatar in 2020 and 2021."

It seemed like whatever point I raised, Jassim had facts and figures to counter it. He kept on with the onslaught.

"I'd like to point out that the Equidem report was based on interviews with sixty workers – sixty. And according to their own report, nineteen of those sixty praised the labor practices of the contractors they worked for. That means that the negative allegations contained in their report was based on forty-one workers, much of it based on hearsay accusations, out of approximately thirty thousand workers who worked on World Cup projects.

I'd hardly call that a comprehensive study."

* * *

When Mary and I got back to our hotel after the interview, I asked her what she thought.

"Jassim was quite convincing," she said. "My impression is that they had a lot of problems at the start of the construction phase, but worked hard to fix them and get rid of the bad contractors."

"That's what I thought too," I said. "I noticed that you were talking to Fatima at the end of the meeting while Jassim and I were wrapping up. What were you two talking about?"

"She started off by complimenting me on my outfit," Mary said, "but then she asked who else we were meeting with. I told her we were meeting with FIFA and one of the contractors tomorrow. She said she was glad we were planning to do a balanced report."

"I also told her we were heading to Saudi Arabia after that to meet with the Khan brothers."

"And what did she say about that?" I asked.

"She said to be very, *very* careful."

CHAPTER 4

The next day, Mary and I met with the General Secretary of the Qatar Football Association and I asked the same questions that I'd asked the representatives of the World Cup Supreme Committee.

"I'm not in a position to answer those questions," he said, "because I was not on the selection committee. You must realize that not all members of FIFA get a vote. It is only those who are members of the Executive Committee who decide what countries get to host the World Cup."

However, he did address the criticism that Qatar didn't have a competitive team, even though as host, they automatically qualified for the event.

"We are the Asian champions," he said. "We have been building for this for a long time. Eighteen years ago, we founded the Aspire Academy with the aim of finding and nurturing the best talent in football and other sports. We started scouting prospects at eleven years of age and brought in the top coaches from around the world to help them develop. We won the Under-19 AFC cup in 2014 and later defeated Japan in the 2019 Asian

Cup."

"Yet your team didn't win a single game in this World Cup and failed to get out of the group stage," I countered.

"As did Canada," he said.

Touché.

* * *

Later that afternoon, Mary and I met with a representative from one of the major contractors in building the World Cup stadiums. I asked him for his comments about the allegations of abuse of foreign workers.

"At the start of the construction phase, I heard the rumors that there were some contractors that were abusing their workers," he said. "We were pleased when the SC started cracking down on those contractors and removing them from the projects. They were giving the rest of us, who were following the rules, a bad name."

"So what do you believe were the actual number of workers killed and/or injured on these projects?" I asked.

"I have no idea," he said. "I can verify that *our* company only had a handful, and we've documented them fully. Regarding the overall numbers, my impression is that the International Labor Organization's estimate is probably the most believable. They determined that fifty workers died and another five hundred were injured in 2020."

"And you think the numbers were worse in the years before that?"

"That would seem to be a reasonable assumption," he said, "but I don't have any hard data to support it. That was the problem. No one was keeping track of it in the early days."

* * *

Later that night in the hotel, Mary and I were reviewing our notes.

"Did the U.S. Justice Department really charge fourteen FIFA executives with corruption?" Mary asked.

"Yes," I said. "They found over $150 million in bribes and kickbacks were paid to FIFA officials. Another sixteen officials were eventually charged and two others turned themselves in. The corruption goes back decades. They've documented that the South African government paid a bribe of $10 million dollars to be selected to host the 2010 World Cup."

"What about the World Cups held in Russia and Qatar?"

"Both countries have denied the allegations," I said, "but suspicions remain."

"Boy, FIFA almost sounds like the Mafia. Did they arrest the head of FIFA?"

"Surprisingly, no," I said. "Sepp Blatter was the president of FIFA from 1998 to 2015 and all of this happened under his watch. He wasn't charged, but he was banned from FIFA until at least 2027. Speculation is that he turned a blind eye to the corruption."

"How did the Justice Department discover all of this?" Mary asked.

"They had an informant on the inside. They discovered that Chuck Blazer, the U.S. FIFA Executive Committee member from 1996 to 2013, had taken a bribe in awarding the 2010 World Cup to South Africa. During the investigation, the IRS discovered that he hadn't filed any tax returns for over a decade and he was facing a jail sentence of between 75 and 100 years. He decided to flip and become an informant about all of the other corruption within FIFA."

"Did he ever go to jail?" Mary asked.

"No, he pled guilty, but he died of colorectal cancer before he was sentenced."

"What about all of the others?" Mary asked.

"Fourteen of them were found guilty and forfeited most of the money they had illegally received, but it appears very few actually went to jail. I think it's up to their own countries to determine if they want to take it further. I know there was one executive from South America that was sentenced to nine years in jail and another guy from El Salvador that was sentenced to sixteen months. I don't know how many others actually went to prison."

Mary shook her head in disgust and got up and paced back and forth across our hotel room. "I'm really worried about our interview tomorrow with the Khan brothers. Have you figured out how you're going to approach them?"

I gave a heavy sigh. "I haven't decided. Up until now, we've only been investigating the broad aspects of the corruption, but I'd like nothing better than to nail these guys. I've got the material given to me by Sarah that documents some of their corruption, but I suspect they'll just deny it. I don't have any way of forcing them to disclose their financial records. Without any solid proof, I can't put any of it in a story. If I did, they'd get their lawyers to sue me and the newspaper and take us for all we're worth."

"But we can't just let them get away with it," Mary said. "We have to do something!"

I thought back to the warning Mary had received from Fatima at the Supreme Committee's office to *be very, very careful* when around the Khan brothers. "I'm afraid they might do something worse than just sue us."

CHAPTER 5

The next morning we caught an early morning flight from Doha, Qatar to Riyadh, the Saudi Arabian capital and the location of the Khan brothers' head office. We were scheduled to meet with both of them together, so we were surprised when only Ahmad came into the room.

Ahmad was a big, intimidating man who looked like he could have been a rugby star when he was younger. His eyes were dark and appeared to be suspicious of everything they saw. His demeanor toward me was cold, at best, and when he looked at Mary, he looked absolutely disgusted. He told us that Dawood was busy doing *real work*, but he hoped to be able to join us later.

I tried to soften Ahmad up by initially throwing him some easy questions about the success of their construction projects in Qatar, but it didn't work. He simply pushed one of their brochures across the table toward me saying "I think you'll find all of the information you're looking for in there."

I glanced over at Mary and she seemed quite nervous. Ahmad kept his focus on me and didn't seem to want to acknowledge that she was even in the room.

"We're investigating several allegations of bribery and corruption regarding the construction contracts associated with the Qatar World Cup," I said. I slid a copy of one of the documents that Sarah had provided me across the table toward him.

He didn't even look at the document. "We didn't bribe anyone," he said.

"Then how do you explain this record showing that your company paid one million Saudi Riyal, or the equivalent of over $250,000 U.S. dollars, to the Qatari Football Association?"

He still refused to look at the document. "We didn't bribe anyone," he repeated.

I pushed another document toward him. This was a copy of an email to one of their competitors where it appeared they were fixing the bids on some of the construction contracts.

Once again, he refused to look at the document.

Our staring contest was interrupted when his brother, Dawood, came into the meeting room.

"My sincere apologies for my tardiness," Dawood said. "What have I missed?"

Ahmad stood and started to leave the room, but he whispered something to Dawood when he passed by and he said it loud enough so that everyone could hear. "I told you this was a waste of time," he said, "and someone should tell that whore how a proper woman is supposed to dress."

Mary flinched.

After Ahmad had left the room, Dawood turned toward me and smiled. "My apologies for the abruptness of my brother. He's been having a bad week, but that's no reason for him to take it out on you."

Then Dawood turned toward Mary. "And who would

this beautiful lady be?"

"This is Mary Byrnes, an associate of mine," I said.

Mary seemed to blush a little as Dawood softly and elegantly shook her hand.

"I apologize for my appearance," Mary said. "The airline lost my luggage and the clerk at the store said this would be appropriate attire."

"It is both lovely and appropriate," Dawood said. "My brother is stuck in his old ways and does not want to accept that things are not the way they once were."

The atmosphere had taken on a much more positive tone as soon as Dawood had entered the room, and I hoped this would continue.

"I'm not sure if you remember me from our meeting in Qatar almost a year ago," I said, "but I'm…"

He cut me off before I could finish. "Of course I remember you, Mr. McKenzie. May I call you Andrew? And of course, please call me Dawood. I hear that you've had quite an interesting time of it since we last spoke."

I instantly recalled how charming Dawood had been at our last meeting. He was the exact opposite of his brother. Dawood was tall and thin and not the least bit intimidating, and his eyes were a shimmering blue that seemed to dance as he spoke. But I remembered how I had been fooled by him at our last meeting and was determined not to let his charm get the better of me this time.

"How can I help you?" Dawood asked.

"Unfortunately, we're here investigating the corruption within FIFA," I said, "particularly as it relates to the World Cup held in Qatar."

"Well, there's no disputing the corruption within FIFA," Dawood said. "It was just a matter of time until it all came to light, but what is it you want to ask *me*?"

I slid the same document that I had shown to Ahmad over to Dawood, the one that showed a payment of one million Saudi Riyal to the Qatari Football Association.

"Given the accusations of bribery toward FIFA, this payment of funds from your company appears somewhat suspicious," I said.

Dawood picked up the document and studied it for a few seconds. "Yes, I remember this payment." He pointed to the date. "It was made in 2014 and I authorized it myself. It was a donation to the Qatari Football Association to help them bring in some high-priced coaches to help them with the development of their football team. You have to realize that the 2022 World Cup was not only important to Qatar, but it was also important to all of the countries in the Middle East. We knew the Qatari team was considered weak and we did not want them to be embarrassed on the pitch. If you check, I think you'll find we also made donations to the teams from Saudi Arabia and Tunisia, not only in 2014, but in the next few years as well."

"So you're saying that the payment was not made as a bribe to Qatar to be given favorable treatment in the awarding of construction contracts?" I asked.

Dawood smiled. "Absolutely not. There was no need to bribe anyone. There was so much building to be done in such a short period of time, they were desperate for construction companies such as ours to step forward and help."

I slid the next document toward him, the one with the email showing collusion with another construction company in fixing bids.

Dawood studied this document more intensely, then reached for the phone in the conference room and called someone. A woman appeared at the door a few seconds later. Dawood whispered something to her as he handed her the document and she scurried out of the room.

"I'm having someone in my staff investigate the document you showed me," Dawood said. "I'll have an answer for you before the end of our meeting."

We continued asking Dawood questions for the next twenty minutes and he answered them all. I was debating how much further to push things.

"Surely, you didn't come all of this way to ask me questions that you probably already knew the answers to," he said. "Why don't you ask me what you *really* want to know?"

I looked at Mary and she seemed to be encouraging me to push further, but my throat suddenly felt dry. There was a pitcher of ice-water on a tray on the board room table along with several glasses. I desperately wanted a drink, but I thought back to my last meeting with Dawood from a year ago and wondered if I'd been drugged at that meeting. I would not let it happen again.

As if he read my mind, Dawood got out of his chair and headed to the back of the room. He opened one of the cabinet doors which revealed a small fridge and pulled out three bottles.

"Would you prefer a ginger ale, a Coke, or a bottled water?" he asked both Mary and myself.

Mary took the ginger ale, I took the Coke, and Dawood twisted the cap off of the bottled water for himself. He seemed to sense what we were nervous about.

"So, what else would you like to know?" he asked again as he sat down.

I still didn't know what to do.

"Did you arrange for someone to kill your wife?" Mary suddenly blurted out.

Dawood smiled. "Now, we're finally getting somewhere." He leaned forward in his seat. "No, I did *not* arrange for someone to kill my wife. In fact, for a long time, I was convinced she was killed by your RCMP Superintendent Powell and you guys were just covering it up. Now, I don't know what to believe."

"But I met with your wife," I said. "*She's* the one who told me you were trying to kill her. She's also the one who provided me with the documents I gave you showing the corruption surrounding the World Cup."

"Yes, I know about your little meeting with my wife in that hotel room in Nova Scotia," Dawood said, "but my wife was not the person you think she was."

"She said your marriage was on the rocks and she was trying to escape to North America to get away from you," I said. "She said you drugged all of the people on board that flight, including me, in an attempt to have her killed without anyone finding out."

"It wasn't *me* who drugged all of those people," Dawood said.

"Then who was it?"

"I don't know," he said.

There was a soft knock on the door and the young woman who Dawood had whispered to earlier came in with several pieces of paper in her hand. She handed the papers to Dawood and then left.

Dawood studied them for a while and then put them on the table before me. He seemed surprised and disappointed.

"Here's the *complete* copy of the email you showed me earlier," Dawood said. "In the copy you had, the names of the sender and receiver had been conveniently left off the document. I had one of my assistants pull the entire email from one of our backups."

I read the complete version of the email.

"What does it say?" Mary asked.

"It shows that Ahmad Khan and the president of the other construction company were the recipients," I said.

"Yes, but who sent it?" Mary asked.

I could see the answer in black and white, but it was Dawood who provided the answer.

"My wife."

CHAPTER 6

"I don't' understand," I said. "Why would your wife be writing emails about construction bids?"

"It appears you know very little about my wife," Dawood said. "What did she tell you about us?"

"She told me that you met each other while at university in England and fell madly in love. After you graduated, you got married and you moved back here to work for your father. She said you were an idealist, rejected the ways of your father, and tried to introduce new ways of doing business. She said your marriage encountered problems after a few years here and she was planning to leave you, but you didn't want her to go."

"That's all true," Dawood said.

"She also said you were constantly fighting with your father and your brother about how to run things. Eventually, you caved and became as corrupt as they were."

"That's where you're wrong," Dawood said. She was correct in saying I was constantly fighting with my father and my brother. My father owned 51% of the company and my brother and I owned the other 49%, so I effectively had no control at all. However, when my father passed away, my brother and I inherited his shares and we became equal partners. Except that my wife convinced me to put 10% of my shares in her name, mostly for tax purposes, but also because she was bored and wanted to start working in the company. She became our Director of Administration."

"She didn't tell me that," I said.

"I'm not surprised," Dawood said. "However, my wife was seduced by the new-found power she had and by how much money we were making. It wasn't *me* who became corrupt – it was her – and she started siding with my brother in doing deals under the table. I didn't become aware of it until much later on."

"So, is that why she was trying to get away from you and flee to America?" Mary asked.

"She wasn't running from me," Dawood said. "She was running from my brother. After most of the Executive Committee members from FIFA were found to be corrupt, the authorities started taking a closer look at companies such as ours that had been doing business with FIFA. That's when my brother found out that she'd been altering our records so that *he* became the fall guy for all of their side-deals. And let me assure you, you do *not* want to get on the bad side of my brother."

"So do you think it was your *brother* who drugged all of those people on the plane and had your wife killed?" Mary asked.

"I don't know," Dawood said. "I know my brother felt betrayed by Sarah and was desperate to find her, but I don't think that he would have actually arranged to have her killed."

"You said earlier that your brother was having a particularly bad week. Are the authorities getting close to arresting him for corruption?" I asked.

"No, I don't think the authorities have figured out much of anything yet," Dawood said. "It will probably take them years to determine the full extent of it, if they *ever* do. My wife was quite good at hiding things, as I have since found out. And if she couldn't hide it, she left a trail pointing to someone else, as you have now discovered."

"The reason my brother is having a bad week," Dawood continued, "is because I submitted my resignation two days ago. I'll be leaving the company at the end of the year. He's been trying to get complete control over the business for a long time now."

"Why would you do that?" I asked, "and why would that stress him out?"

"Because I'm tired of fighting with him, so we've now reached a crossroads in the future of our company. My brother is upset because my resignation forces him to purchase my shares in the company and that will cost him close to four billion Saudi Riyal. He only has ninety days to come up with the money and I know he doesn't have it."

"Why wouldn't he be able to raise the funds?" I asked. "He'd be able to use the assets of the company to help finance the deal."

"Because that would trigger an audit of all of our financial records, something he'd obviously want to avoid out of fear they'd discover the fraud that has been going on."

"What happens if he can't come up with the money within ninety days?" I asked.

Dawood smiled. "Then I get to buy him out at the same price. Our share-purchase agreement has a shotgun clause. Either I get 100% control of the company, or he does. I can easily raise the money, but he can't, so I'm the one with my finger on the trigger."

My head was spinning with all of this new information.

"But he's got an even bigger problem than that," Dawood added.

"What could that possibly be?" Mary asked.

Dawood turned toward her. "Before my wife boarded that flight to North America, she moved almost $100 million Saudi Riyal from the company's accounts to hidden offshore accounts. The company is, practically speaking, financially bankrupt. Since my wife is dead, we have no way of knowing where all of that money went."

Except that I knew something that they didn't. Sarah was still alive. Suddenly, I felt like I was going to throw up.

CHAPTER 7

Mary and I flew back to Toronto the next day, or more accurately, very early the next morning. The first leg of the flight left at two in the morning and took us from Riyadh, Saudi Arabia, to Frankfurt, Germany, where we had a three hour layover before the connecting flight to Toronto.

"Are you disappointed with what we discovered on this trip?" Mary asked me, while we waited in the lounge in Frankfurt.

"I think *surprised* would be a more accurate word to use," I said.

"Do you believe everything Dawood told us?" she asked.

I thought for several seconds. "I don't know. He sure was convincing, but Sarah had warned me that he had used his charm at our first meeting to con me and that had almost cost me my life. Now I don't know who or what to believe."

Mary looked concerned. "Yeah, me too. What does this do to your story?"

"I'm not sure," I said. "I've got more information

about the corruption within FIFA, but other journalists have already written about that. I was hoping that I'd uncover enough evidence to have Dawood charged with corruption and the murders of all of those people on board that flight, but that's where I failed."

"Do you think it was actually his brother, Ahmad?" Mary asked. "He certainly came across as a scary son-of-a-bitch. I could see him killing anyone who gets in his way."

"Maybe," I said, "but something about that theory doesn't make sense. If Sarah had actually moved $100 million Saudi Riyal to hidden offshore accounts, why would Ahmad try to have her killed? Without her, he has no way of getting back the money she stole."

"How much is that in Canadian dollars?" Mary asked.

"About $36 million Canadian," I said, "or about $27 million U.S. dollars."

"Maybe he didn't know that Sarah had stolen the money at that point," Mary said. "He might have just tried to kill her out of revenge for setting him up as the fall guy for all of their shady deals."

Mary was right. The timing was key. I checked the time and realized that Dawood should now be in his office back in Riyadh. I was a little surprised when he took my call and I wasted no time in asking the key question.

"I don't know when Ahmad found out the money was missing," Dawood said. "I didn't discover it until after I got back in the office after the completion of the World Cup. If Ahmad knew before that, he didn't tell me, but as I've already told you, both he and Sarah had been hiding things from me for a while."

* * *

As Mary and I flew from Frankfurt to Toronto, I realized I had a lot more work to do before I solved this case. Mary quickly fell asleep, but my mind was churning with various questions and theories.

Theory #1: Ahmad Khan had arranged to have Sarah killed for stealing $100 million Saudi Riyal from their company and setting him up as the fall-guy for their shady deals. His goal of getting revenge against Sarah overshadowed everything else, and he had considered the rest of the passengers onboard Flight 059 as merely collateral damage.

Theory #2: Dawood Khan had once again used his charm to convince me that he was an honest business man, but was actually a master manipulator. He was now in a position to gain total control over their construction company and have both Sarah and Ahmad out of the picture.

Theory #3: Superintendent Powell and I had been duped by Sarah. She hadn't been disillusioned by her husband's fall into corruption. It had been the other way around.

I knew I had to question Sarah again to get to the bottom of this, but I had no idea where she was. I decided to contact Superintendent Powell to get that information.

CHAPTER 8

Mary and I spent one more day together when we got back to Toronto, but then she had to fly back to Gander to resume her job as an ICU nurse.

I filed a story about the corruption I'd discovered surrounding the World Cup, but my editor said there wasn't enough there to justify putting it in the newspaper. He was right. Other reporters and other newspapers had already covered the corruption within FIFA.

As per our agreement, I hadn't spoken to Superintendent Powell in almost a year. However, we had also agreed I could contact him if I came up with enough evidence to have Dawood Khan charged with the murders of all of those passengers onboard Flight 059. He'd said he'd pull Sarah out of witness protection to come back to testify at the trial, if required. But now I needed to contact him to let him know of the possibility that we'd both been duped by Sarah.

I was surprised when I got the *"number no longer in service"* message when I tried to call him. Searching for him on the internet only returned his old contact info at the RCMP, which was outdated and useless. And since I was well-known as the reporter who had crucified him and the RCMP in the press over allowing Sarah to commit suicide while in their custody, no one at the RCMP was willing to help me.

I eventually tracked down an address and a telephone number for Superintendent Powell's wife, Kathleen. I assumed it was listed under his wife's name because he was now trying to live off the grid. The address was for a small acreage near Enderby, British Columbia. I called and left a voice-mail.

Since no one called me back, I tried again a couple of days later, but was forced to leave another voice-mail. I tried again the day after that and this time, his wife answered. I explained who I was and told her that it was extremely important for Superintendent Powell to call me back. There was silence on the other end of the phone for the longest time.

"Haven't you already done enough to destroy his reputation?" she cried into the phone. "For Christ sake, just let the man rest in peace!".

Then she hung up.

Rest in peace, I thought to myself. Was he dead? What the hell had happened?

I thought back to the old saying *"The only way three people can keep a secret is if two of them are dead."*

And now there were only two of us left. Sarah Khan and myself.

CHAPTER 9

My next call was to RCMP Inspector Brad Taylor. He had been Superintendent Powell's partner in the investigation of Flight 059 and I thought we had developed a pretty good rapport. Unfortunately, I only got to leave a voice-mail with him.

When he still hadn't returned my call by the next day, I decided to fly to Ottawa and camp outside of RCMP headquarters. Through various sources, I had managed to determine that he was onsite, and I had decided a face-to-face meeting was the best way to tell him about the new information I had gathered. When I saw Inspector Taylor leaving the building, I followed him to his car. He sensed he was being followed and turned.

"What do *you* want?" he asked.

"I have something important to tell you," I said, "and I need your help."

He kept walking toward his car. "I'm not interested in *anything* you have to say."

He opened his car door and was just about to get in when I said, "Sarah Khan is alive."

To my surprise, he still got in his car and started it. I thought maybe he hadn't heard me and was just going to drive away, but then he powered down his driver-side window.

"What the fuck are you talking about?"

I maneuvered around the front of his car and he unlocked the passenger door. I climbed in.

He put his foot on the gas and we quickly exited the parking lot. "You're persona non grata around here and I shouldn't even be seen talking to you."

He was right. No one within the RCMP was willing to give me the time of day after I'd destroyed Powell's reputation in the media.

Taylor drove for a few minutes, then stopped in an almost-empty parking lot behind an industrial building. "Explain yourself," he said.

"Sarah's suicide was fabricated by Powell in order to get her into witness protection," I said. "When he questioned her almost a year ago, he came to the same conclusion that I had – that her husband had planned to have her killed onboard that flight and that *he* was the one who was really responsible for the deaths of all those people. Powell figured her husband would continue to come after her if he thought she was still alive."

"He wouldn't have done that without telling me," Taylor said. "I was his partner. We'd worked together for over twenty years."

"Powell told me he thought the only way this would work was if we kept it a secret," I said. "The fewer people, the better."

"Then why would he tell you? You're a *fucking* reporter."

"Because he said the only way this would work was if he took the blame for her suicide. And he needed me to crucify him in the press or else people would think the police were covering something up."

Taylor looked like he was still having trouble believing what I was telling him. "Why would he do that? He'd been with the force for over thirty-five years and had a spotless record."

"He told me he was going to be retiring soon anyway," I said. "I think Sarah won him over and he was looking for a way to help her. She can be quite convincing."

"So why are you telling me this now?" he asked.

"Because I think Sarah may have conned us all," I said. "A year ago, Sarah gave me evidence documenting her husband's corruption. Powell told me if I dug up enough evidence to have her husband charged with corruption and murdering the people onboard Flight 059, then he'd pull her out of witness protection so she could come back and testify at her husband's trial."

"I just got back from the Middle East," I continued. "It turns out her husband wasn't the corrupt one, it was actually Sarah and her husband's brother, Ahmad, who were involved in the shady deals. Except she double-crossed him as well. Sarah transferred about $100 million Saudi Riyal to an offshore account and was fleeing to North America to get away from Ahmad. I think *he* might have been the one who killed all of those people onboard that flight. I think he was also trying to kill Sarah."

Taylor thought for a while, trying to comprehend everything I was telling him. "What do you want from me?" he asked.

"First," I said, "I need to know what happened to Powell."

Taylor's face fell. "He committed suicide," he said. "He and his wife were hounded by the press here in

Ottawa for months after the incident, *thanks to you*. He told me they couldn't take it anymore. They sold their house and moved to some place in British Columbia. No one was supposed to know where they went, but some reporter in B.C. found him and the stories started all over again. His wife, Kathleen, told me that he became more and more depressed."

"So what happened?" I asked.

"Kathleen told me they used to go on long hikes in the mountains to get away from everybody. One day, he went for a hike by himself, climbed to the top of a ridge and shot himself with his own gun. They found his body and his gun at the bottom of a cliff."

"Why didn't I hear anything about this?" I asked.

"Kathleen blames you guys in the press for causing his death," he said. "The last thing she wanted was another media circus around his suicide and she begged us to keep it quiet. We buried the report."

"Do you think he *really* committed suicide?" I asked.

"I did at the time," he said.

We both sat in silence for a while.

"I'm wondering if Sarah Khan might have killed him," I said, "and just made it appear like a suicide."

"Yeah, I just started wondering about that as well," Taylor said. "If she *is* the con artist that you say she is, she'd want to eliminate anyone who knows that she's still alive." He gave me a concerned look. "And you know who that means she's coming for next."

CHAPTER 10

I knew exactly what Inspector Taylor was saying and I knew I would be a pretty easy target. That meant I had to find Sarah before she found me.

"Do you think you can find out what name she's using now and where the Witness Protection Program moved her to?" I asked.

"That will be difficult," he said. "Those files are sealed, for obvious reasons. Even as an RCMP officer, I doubt I'll be given access, but I'll try."

Taylor called me the following afternoon.

"I got shut down," he said. "According to official records, she was never even *in* the Witness Protection Program."

"Isn't that the standard RCMP answer to any inquiries," I asked.

"Yes, but I even asked the new Superintendent to look into it as well and he came back with nothing. But I did pull the police report on Powell's suicide. Everything appears legit. The cause of death was a contact GSW (Gun Shot Wound) to the head, only *his* fingerprints were found on the gun found close to his body, and his wife had indicated he'd been severely depressed in the days leading up to his disappearance."

"Did he leave any kind of note?" I asked.

"No, but his wife said he'd told her that *he was really, really sorry for the pain he'd caused her* when they went to bed the night before. She said he was gone when she woke up the next morning. Some hikers discovered his body a day later at the bottom of a cliff."

"Did they do an autopsy?" I asked.

"No, his wife asked them not to, and since all evidence pointed to a suicide, they agreed to her request."

"Who identified the body?"

"His wife, Kathleen. And by the way, everything I'm telling you is off the record. I better not see anything about this in your newspaper."

"Agreed," I said.

"So what are you going to do now?" Taylor asked.

I had no idea.

CHAPTER 11

My editor at the newspaper told me he thought the story about what had happened onboard Flight 059 had run its course, even when I told him that Powell had committed suicide. He told me to just let the man rest in peace and he put me on new assignments.

However, I'd never told him that Sarah Khan was still alive and that I'd made up the whole story about her suicide. If I did, I'm sure he would have fired me. The newspaper would lose all credibility if it became known that they were affiliated with a reporter who had fabricated a story.

I was now second-guessing myself for letting Powell talk me into going along with the whole scheme. Secrets had a habit of coming back to bite you in the ass when they came out, and they *always* seemed to come out eventually.

But at the time, I thought I was doing the right thing. Powell had convinced me that this was the only way to protect Sarah from her dangerous husband. He was also the one willing to face the shit-storm from our fabrication. Using the evidence Sarah had given me, the plan was that I'd dig up more evidence to have her husband charged. Sarah would come out of hiding to testify at his trial and rather than being admonished for fabricating a story, he'd be the hero cop and I'd be heralded as the reporter who'd worked with the police to uncover the *real* culprit.

Except that I now felt I was standing on shaky ground with the possibility that Sarah had conned both of us. Powell was now dead and I was stuck with keeping the secret of what we'd done. Sure, I'd told Inspector Taylor, but I'm not sure he really believed me. I suspected that he thought of me as either a liar or a fool.

But I couldn't let it go. When the newspaper sent me to Vancouver to report on another story, I decided to take a slight diversion instead of flying directly back to Toronto. I changed my return flight to have a twelve hour layover in Kelowna. If anyone at the newspaper questioned it, I would tell them it was so I could have a brief visit with some friends. It wouldn't cost the newspaper anything extra; in fact, my indirect flights were actually cheaper.

I took the earliest available flight from Vancouver to Kelowna. I hadn't called Kathleen Powell to let her know I was coming. If I had, I'm sure she would have refused to see me and this was something I had to do in person, not over the phone.

It was about an hour's drive from the Kelowna airport to her place near Enderby and as I made the scenic drive, I planned out what I was going to say. First, I would give my condolences for her loss. Then I would tell her what her husband and I had done and why. I would tell her that I now believed that we'd both be duped by Sarah Khan, and then I would ask Kathleen for her forgiveness. I wasn't sure she'd absolve me, but that didn't matter.

She deserved to know the truth.

I was using the GPS on my phone, which I had plugged into the screen on my rental car, to navigate my way there. Just outside of Enderby, I turned off the main highway onto a narrow, paved road that wound its way up a small mountain. Every half-mile or so, there would be a dirt road that would feed off into the bush. People who lived up here obviously were looking for privacy.

When the GPS indicated that I'd reached my destination, I couldn't see a road or a house anywhere. I slowed the car down to a crawl and saw a dirt laneway that led into the trees a few hundred yards ahead. It had a For Sale sign at the end of the laneway. I turned onto the road and continued along as it meandered and climbed further up the mountain.

Finally, the trees cleared and I found myself in front of a two-story rustic lodge that looked like it had been built right into the side of the mountain. It looked old and dated, but impressive none-the-less.

I got out of the car and knocked on the door of the lower level. When I didn't get a response, I climbed the stairs that led up to the deck that surrounded the house on three sides. I knocked on the door on that level, but didn't get a response there either. I yelled "Hello, is anybody home?" into the wilderness, but my call just faded into the trees.

As I spun around looking in all directions, I could see why someone would want to live here. It was a postcard view of huge evergreens cascading down to the valley below, then rising again to more mountains on the other side. The top level of the house was almost all windows, so you'd be looking at this view no matter which room you were in.

I couldn't stop myself from peering in the windows.

The place looked lived in, but there didn't appear to be anyone around right now.

When I walked around to the far side of the deck, I saw two Adirondack chairs with a small wooden table between them. There was a book on the table – my book – with an envelope inserted into it being used as a bookmark. When I opened the book, I could see the envelope had the RCMP logo on it and Superintendent Powell's name and address. I was obviously in the right place.

I waited for about ten minutes more before deciding to get back in my car and head into Enderby to get a coffee and something to eat. I had no idea how long it would be until Kathleen came back home.

I had just made my way onto the twisty, paved road toward the town when a car passed me going the other way. Since the road was so narrow, we both had to slow down to a crawl to get by each other. I was convinced it was Kathleen and watched in my rear-view mirror as she continued along her way. Sure enough, she turned onto the dirt road I had just exited.

I continued down the paved road until the next dirt roadway, then used it to turn around and head back. When I got back to the house, I could see Kathleen parked in front of the garage, unloading groceries from her vehicle. I stopped my car about twenty paces away from hers, as there was a circular laneway in front of the house.

I had never met her before, and I was surprised by her appearance. Based on our brief phone conversation, I had pictured someone weak and frail, but this woman looked anything but. She was tall – almost six feet – thin and wiry. She looked like she could run a marathon, even though the lines on her face indicated she'd be over sixty years of age.

When I got out of my car, she yelled over, "if you're here about the house, you'll have to make an appointment with the agent. His number's on the sign at the end of the driveway".

"I'm not here about the house," I said as I approached.

She reached back into the car and pulled out another bag of groceries. She also placed a revolver on the roof of the car, in plain view. Message received.

"Whoa," I said as I came to an abrupt halt. "There's no need for a gun. I'm not here to hurt you, I'm just here to talk."

"Then do your talking from over there."

"My name is Andrew McKenzie. I'm a reporter with the Toronto Star. We spoke briefly on the phone."

She squinted her eyes at me and picked up the gun. She didn't point it at me, but I sensed she wanted to. "I'm not interested in anything *you* have to say."

"Please," I said. "It's important. I think you'll want to hear what I have to tell you. It might explain why your husband did what he did."

She studied me for what seemed like an eternity. Finally, she put the gun in her jacket pocket, picked up one of the bags of groceries, came over and handed it to me. "Carry this up to the kitchen for me. There's frozen stuff in there and I have to get it into the freezer."

She picked up two grocery bags herself and led the way up the stairs to the kitchen. She quickly put away her groceries, while I watched.

I felt nervous around her and tried to lighten the mood. "I can't tell you how happy I was to see you put away that gun." I gave her a Cheshire grin.

"I did a risk assessment on you and determined that I

didn't *need* the gun. I figure I could take you out with my bare hands if I need to."

I laughed, but she wasn't smiling, and I was convinced she was right.

"Are you a cop?" I asked.

"Not anymore," she said. "But I was an RCMP officer for almost twenty years. That's where Simon and I met. When he became the Superintendent and effectively my boss, we decided it was best if I left the force, so I started working in intelligence in another organization."

"What organization was that?" I asked.

"That's on a need to know basis, and *you* don't need to know."

After putting her groceries away, she pulled two water bottles from the fridge and threw one to me. "We can talk out on the deck," she said, pointing outside. "I'll give you ten minutes."

I didn't think I could tell her everything I needed to in that amount of time, so I gave her the *Reader's Digest* version. First, I gave her my condolences for her loss. Then I told her that her husband had devised the plan to fake Sarah's death and get her into the Witness Protection Program. I was his accomplice in fabricating the story in the press.

"Simon would never do that," she said, "but if he did, he would have told me."

"Your husband told me that it was critical that we keep this a secret from *everyone*," I said. "He didn't tell his partner at the RCMP and I didn't tell my editor. The only three people who knew about the plan was him, me and Sarah Khan."

"I *still* don't believe you," Kathleen said. "If this was his plan, then why would he kill himself?"

"That's one of the things I wanted to talk to you about," I said. "I've now discovered that Sarah may have conned both your husband and myself. I don't believe she is the innocent victim she portrayed herself to be." I took a deep breath. "Do you think there's any chance that your husband may have been murdered, rather than having committed suicide?"

She stared at me while she processed what I'd just asked her.

"I was told that you requested that they not do an autopsy," I continued. "Why not?"

It took a long time before she replied. "Because all evidence suggested that he'd blown his own head off. I've investigated enough suicides before to know what one looks like. I just wanted him to be able to rest in peace."

"Had he been depressed?" I asked.

"The pressure put on him by you and your cronies in the press had been relentless," she said. "It was wearing us down. That's why we moved out here from Ottawa. People out here tend to mind their own business, but then a local reporter figured out who we were and it started all over again."

"But he was a strong man," I said. "Do you really think it got to him enough for him to take his own life?"

"Simon was the strongest man I'd ever met," she said, "but something was bothering him. The night before he left, he told me that he'd done something terribly wrong. He said he never intended for me to get hurt and he asked for my forgiveness. I asked what he'd done, but he said it was better if I didn't know." She turned her head and looked out over the valley stretching out below us. "When I woke up the next morning, he was gone."

She continued to stare out into the wilderness for a

long time, either thinking about what I'd just told her, or reminiscing about her last hours with her husband, or both.

"I think it's time for you to leave," she said.

Before I left, I told her again how sorry I was for her loss and my role in the tragic sequence of events. I'm not sure she forgave me, but I felt better for telling her the truth.

I asked her not to tell anyone else what I'd told her, at least not until I could find Sarah Khan. "If word gets out that I fabricated the story, I'll lose my job," I said.

She shook her head in disgust. "You *should* lose your job."

I started to respond, but then stopped, because I knew she was right.

CHAPTER 12

After leaving Kathleen's place, I drove to Kelowna to catch my flight back to Toronto. The first leg took me to Calgary, then onto a red-eye flight that got into Toronto about six the next morning. During the flight, I wondered whether Kathleen had believed what I'd told her. I got my answer about a week later when Inspector Taylor called me.

"I heard you visited Kathleen Powell," he said.

"I did," I replied, "and I told her the same thing I told you. I don't know if she believed me or not."

"Well you must have made *some* kind of impression," he said. "She asked them to take another look at her husband's case to verify that it was a suicide and not a murder."

"And what did they find?"

"This is totally off the record," Taylor said.

"Agreed."

"Given the amount of time that's elapsed, all they could really do was review the evidence gathered at the time," Taylor said. "They confirmed that it still looked

49

like a suicide. He was shot with Powell's own gun from close range and his fingerprints were the only ones found on the gun, but they did find something strange."

"What's that?"

"There were multiple sets of footprints at the top of the hill where he pulled the trigger."

"Meaning there was someone else with him at the time," I said.

"Maybe," Taylor said. "The extra set of footprints could have been made any time between when the incident occurred and when the body was found. The second set of footprints could be totally unrelated to his suicide. The trail is a popular one used by hikers, so someone could have just stopped there on the trail to take a picture."

"Wouldn't they have seen his body?" I asked.

"No, because when he shot himself, his body fell almost eighty feet down to the gorge below. The only way we know that's where it happened is because it's directly above where his body was found and there was some blood splatter found on the ground where we believe he took his life. The blood splatter matched Powell's blood type."

"Will they exhume the body to do an autopsy?" I asked.

"They can't," Taylor said. "His body was cremated after the initial investigation was completed."

"What about the second set of footprints?" I asked.

"All we know is what was captured by pictures taken by the investigating officers at the time," Taylor said. "One set of footprints matched the hiking boots worn by Powell. The other set were made by a women's size 7 Adidas brand running shoe, but that's a popular shoe sold by several stores in the area."

"What size of shoe does Sarah Khan wear?" I asked.

"I have no idea," Taylor said.

I thought for several seconds. "How did Kathleen Powell take the news?" I asked.

"I don't know," Taylor said. "I wasn't the one interacting with her. All I know is that she asked us to review the initial findings, and after the review, the case was closed again verifying the same cause of death – Death by Suicide."

"Have you dug up any more information about where Sarah Khan was placed in the Witness Protection Program or what name she's going by these days?" I asked.

"No," Taylor said. "I've been shut down no matter who I ask. The official line is that she was never even *in* the program. There's nothing more I can do."

CHAPTER 13

I knew I had to find a way to track down Sarah Khan, but I had no idea how to do it, mostly because I wasn't sure that anyone other than me really believed she was still alive. Inspector Taylor didn't believe it, even when I confessed and told him what Powell and I had done. I'm sure I'd put some doubts in Kathleen Powell's mind, but now that the police had confirmed that her husband's death was a suicide, I had no idea what she was thinking these days.

I was even starting to doubt myself. Maybe Powell had conned me when he'd said he'd put Sarah into the Witness Protection Program. Maybe she really *did* die when he was interrogating her and this was just his way of creating an elaborate scheme, with my help, to pass it off as a suicide rather than a death occurring while in his custody.

I knew the only way to confirm whether Sarah was still alive was to get a look at her autopsy report. They had done one when we all thought she had died by poisoning after being interrogated by Superintendent Powell. I had requested it at the time, but the RCMP has closed ranks and refused to release it. I hadn't really pushed that hard, because it allowed me to write my stories alleging that this was a huge cover-up of their incompetence in allowing Sarah's death while in their custody.

Unfortunately, I didn't have enough clout to get the RCMP to release Sarah's autopsy report. But the newspaper did, and they had lawyers on staff who filed motions under the *Access to Information Act* on a regular basis.

To do this, I decided I would have to come clean with Chuck, my editor. I would tell him about the scheme that Powell had come up with almost a year earlier to get Sarah into the Witness Protection Program, and my role in fabricating the whole story. I would also tell him that I now thought that both Powell and myself had been duped by Sarah.

I made an appointment to see Chuck, and as I waited outside his office, I rehearsed the exact lines I was going to say. I would finally be released from the pressure of carrying around this enormous secret.

But there's a funny thing about secrets. I've seen it happen numerous times when politicians call press conferences to come clean about past indiscretions. They always seem to go off script. They just seem to replace one lie or secret with another one and things snowball from there. It turned out I'm not much different. I couldn't believe the words that came out my own mouth.

"I need the newspaper's help in accessing Sarah Khan's autopsy report," I said.

"I thought that story was over with months ago," Chuck said. "Why would you want that now?"

"Because I think Superintendent Powell might have conned us," I said. "I think they might have faked her death and moved her into their Witness Protection

Program." I conveniently left out my role in that scheme.

"Why would he do that?" Chuck asked. "We, or more specifically, *you*, raked him over the coals in the press. You caused him and the RCMP a lot of embarrassment in the process. You forced him to resign in disgrace."

"Yes, and now he's apparently committed suicide, except that I'm not so sure it *was* a suicide. I'm thinking that Sarah might have murdered him. That's why I need to verify whether she's still alive or not, and I need access to her autopsy report to do that."

Chuck stared at me for several seconds. "What are you not telling me?" he asked.

"Nothing," I said. I held his stare for a few seconds, but eventually had to break eye contact. Lying to someone you respect is not easy.

"This will take months," Chuck finally said. "We'll request the records, they'll deny our request, then we'll appeal. I have no idea whether we'll ever *really* get access."

"I think we should try," I said.

He shuffled the papers on his desk while he thought about it. "Okay, I'll start the process," he said, "but you continue to work on the other stories I've assigned you in the meantime. This is just back-burner stuff."

"Agreed," I said.

I guess I'm a better liar than I thought.

CHAPTER 14

Nothing much happened over the next three weeks. I worked on my other assignments as Chuck had told me to do. But I couldn't get this case out of my mind. Then I received a call very early one morning.

"Is this Mr. McKenzie from the Toronto Star?" a woman asked.

"Yes it is," I said. "Who's calling?"

"Please hold for Mr. Khan," she said.

A few seconds later, Dawood Khan came on the line.

"Mr. McKenzie, sorry for calling you so early but I received a very strange letter from your government, and I'm hoping you can explain it," he said.

"I will if I can," I said. "What was in the letter?"

"Your newspaper has apparently requested access to my wife's autopsy report, and as per their standard procedure, they say they contact the next of kin – in this case, me – to find out whether I have any objection to them releasing the report. They say they also contact all other affected parties, in this case, the police, to determine if they have any objections to the release of this document. I find it ironic that my lawyer has an outstanding request to obtain a copy of the same autopsy report, which has been denied for almost a year now. It appears that the left hand of your police force over there has no idea what the right hand is doing. But my question to you is, why is your newspaper submitting this request now?"

I debated how much to tell him. I hadn't realized that he would be made aware of the newspaper's request.

"It's a long story," I said.

"I have the time," he said matter-of-factly.

"First of all," I said, "the newspaper has also been asking for access to the autopsy report from day one, but it has always been denied saying it was part of an ongoing investigation. Now that the RCMP have closed the case, we're now making the request through the *Access to Information Act*."

I hoped that would satisfy him. It didn't.

"Are you saying you don't think my wife committed suicide?" he asked.

I took a deep breath. "There is speculation that Superintendent Powell may have faked your wife's death and moved her into the Witness Protection Program. There's a chance that your wife might still be alive."

There was a long pause. "Couldn't that just be verified one way or the other by interrogating Superintendent Powell?"

"That's not possible," I said.

"Why not?"

"Because he's dead."

There was another long pause. "How convenient," he said. "If my wife is really in the Witness Protection Program, who are they trying to protect her from?"

"From you and your brother."

"Do you really think I would try to kill my wife?"

"I did at one time," I said. "Your wife convinced me and Superintendent Powell that she was innocent and that you were the corrupt one, but I've since discovered that she can be quite the con artist."

"It's about time you finally opened your eyes to see what has been *really* going on," he said.

He had a point.

"So what are you going to do?" I asked.

"Well, since neither you or your Canadian police force seem to be able to track her down, I'm planning to go to Canada to try to find her myself."

"Are you sure that's a good idea?" I asked. "First, we're not even sure she's still alive. Second, if she is, she could be anywhere by now. She might have even fled to a different country. How will you find her?"

"I won't be coming alone," he said. "I have people who are good at finding people who don't want to be found."

That sounded ominous.

"What about your brother?" I asked. "Will he be coming as well?"

"Not with me," he said. "I haven't spoken to Ahmad in quite a while. But he might actually be one step ahead of us. I found out this morning that he boarded a flight to Canada two days ago."

That sounded even more ominous.

CHAPTER 15

Two days later, I got a call from an unidentified caller as I was driving on the Don Valley Expressway in Toronto. My cell phone had a Bluetooth connection to the system in my car, so I could answer hands-free.

"Hello?" I said.

No one spoke for several seconds, so I figured it was a telemarketer and was about to hang up.

"I hear you're looking for me," the voice said.

I instantly recognized Sarah's voice and nearly swerved into another car.

"I suggest you drop your search, for your own good," she said.

"You know I can't do that," I said.

There was another long pause. "Look, I like you. You seem like a nice guy, but if you keep looking for me, something bad is going to happen to you or your loved ones. Consider this a warning."

"Did you kill Superintendent Powell?" I asked.

"I heard that he committed suicide," she said. "Why would you think I had anything to do with it?"

"Were you there with him when he died?" I asked.

"You're making a mistake if you keep going down this path," Sarah said. "Powell made a mistake too. I gave him a choice to rectify the situation, and I think he made the right choice. I suggest you heed this warning."

"Where are you?" I asked, but she had already ended the call.

I now had an answer to my first question. Sarah was, in fact, still alive. But she hadn't given me the opportunity to warn her that both her husband, Dawood, and his brother, Ahmad, were also looking for her.

So I now had a new question. Would she still be alive by the time I found her?

CHAPTER 16

On the following Sunday morning, I fired up my laptop preparing for a Zoom call with Mary Byrnes. Mary and I hadn't seen each other in person since our trip to Qatar and Saudi Arabia. It's difficult keeping a romance going long-distance, so we both really cherished our video chats that we did every Sunday morning. And I was particularly looking forward to my trip to Newfoundland to see her in person in a couple of weeks.

I could see the strain on Mary's face as soon as she appeared on the screen. "What's wrong?" I asked.

"There's someone here with me," Mary said.

Suddenly, another face appeared on the screen as she leaned into view with her hand on Mary's shoulder. It was Sarah.

"Hi Andrew. Nice to see you again. I just dropped in to see Mary here this morning to remind you of our deal. You stop your search for me and Mary gets to continue offering her Newfoundland hospitality to everyone who crosses her path."

"Don't you dare hurt her!" I screamed into my computer screen, but I knew there was nothing I could do to stop her.

"I have no intention of hurting her," Sarah said, "provided you keep up your end of the bargain. Mary and I have become quite close friends over the last hour or so. She told me about your recent trip to Saudi Arabia to meet my husband and everything you discovered on that trip."

I could see the fear in Mary's eyes as Sarah spoke.

"Please don't hurt her," I begged. "I'll do whatever you want, just don't hurt her."

Sarah ignored my plea and just kept talking. "But it appears that you haven't been totally honest with poor Mary here, have you? What kind of a relationship can you have with someone if you can't be totally honest with the one you love? Trust me, Andrew, I know all about what secrets can do to a relationship."

I watched as Sarah slowly moved her hand from Mary's shoulder on to her neck. Then she reached up with her other hand and removed one of her earrings. She held the tip of the pin on her earring close to Mary's neck, and I remembered back to how Sarah had killed her bodyguard on the plane using the poison in her earrings.

"Please!" I screamed.

Sarah looked me directly in the eye through the computer screen and then slowly replaced her earring.

"I'm going to leave you two now," Sarah said. "It appears you have a lot to talk about. But remember, I can easily come back to finish this – anywhere – anytime."

Sarah quickly vanished from my vision through the computer screen. In the background, I heard a door slam. Mary broke down and wept.

"Mary, are you okay?" I asked.

She just continued to cry and cry with big heaving sobs. Finally, she seemed like she was starting to regain her composure.

"Is what she said true?" Mary asked.

"Yes," I said.

I decided to tell Mary everything. How Superintendent Powell had faked Sarah's suicide and moved her into the Witness Protection Program, and how I had participated by covering it up in the press. "At the time, I thought I was doing the right thing," I said.

"But how could you have kept that a secret from *me*?" Mary asked.

"I don't know," I said. "I realize now that it was a mistake."

I could see Mary's expression grow colder as I watched her and realized at that moment that our relationship had suffered a serious blow.

"Look, I know I'm supposed to fly out to see you in a couple of weeks," I said, "but I'm going to immediately book a flight to get there as soon as I can."

"Don't bother," she said. "I don't think you should come. Ever."

Then I watched as she reached up and clicked the button to end the Zoom call.

CHAPTER 17

The next morning I told Chuck, my editor, that we should withdraw our request to gain access to Sarah Khan's autopsy report.

"Give it more time," Chuck said. "I told you it could take up to a year before we get to see it. There's a lot of bureaucracy to work through."

"There's no point," I said. "I know the autopsy report has been faked."

"How do you know that?" Chuck asked.

"Because Sarah Khan is still alive. I've spoken to her."

He looked at me in disbelief.

"Superintendent Powell faked her death and secretly moved her into Witness Protection," I said. I hesitated to tell Chuck about my role in this sleight of hand.

Chuck's face lit up. "I think this just turned into an even *bigger* story. Do you know where she is?"

"Yes," I said. "She's in Newfoundland, but there's a problem. She said she'd come after me and the ones I love if I keep searching for her."

"Come on," he said. "This is not the first time you've received threats to back off a story. If we backed off every time someone threatened us, we'd never publish anything."

"I don't think these are just idle threats. She's already threatened Mary's life." I told him about my recent video chat. "I think she's serious – deadly serious."

Chuck sat down at his desk and contemplated what I 'd just told him.

"There's something else I need to tell you," I said. I'd been carrying around this secret for far too long and it was causing me nothing but trouble. I told him how Powell had involved me in his plan to fake Sarah's death and how I'd gone along with it.

Chuck's mouth hung open in amazement. "Why would you do that?"

"At the time, I thought I was doing the right thing," I said, "but I discovered when I was in Saudi Arabia that Sarah had played us all for fools."

I half-expected that Chuck would scream obscenities at me and fire me on the spot, but he just stared at me as if he was in shock. "I'm sorry," I said.

When I left his office, I had no idea what he was going to do. I got my answer about twenty minutes later when the Head of Personnel and a security guard showed up at my desk.

Hardly a word was spoken. I knew why they were there. I handed them my security card, my laptop and the keys to my desk. I took my personal items, including my picture of Mary, and placed them into a small box they had brought with them. This job had been my whole life for as long as I could remember.

As the security guard escorted me from the premises, an eerie silence fell over the building. It was as if all of the conversations and all of the phones had suddenly been put on mute. I felt the stares of countless pairs of eyes on me as I walked out of the building, but no one would make actual eye contact with me.

A year ago, I made a decision to keep a secret thinking I was doing the right thing. But that secret had now cost me my job and the trust of a woman whose love and support had helped me make it through one of the scariest events of my life.

I had no idea how I was going to dig myself out of the hole I'd managed to put myself in. I'd been such a fool. Little did I know that I hadn't even reached bottom yet.

CHAPTER 18

I crashed on my couch that night after making a major dent in an old bottle of scotch that I had been saving for a special occasion. This wasn't the occasion I'd had in mind when I'd bought the bottle ten years earlier, but it was the only booze I had, so I decided to crack the seal. I had also turned off my cell phone after receiving several calls and texts from colleagues at the Toronto Star who'd heard about me being fired.

The next morning, I woke up to a media frenzy and a throbbing headache. The Toronto Star had published the story about what Powell and I had done a year earlier. It was the lead story on every Canadian news channel and was even being picked up by several international news agencies.

The Star had issued an apology and made it clear that I had been fired for my part in fabricating the story of Sarah Khan's suicide. The RCMP had closed ranks and were neither confirming or denying the story.

Everyone was now trying to find out where Sarah was hiding. There were numerous reports of her being seen in every province from coast to coast.

When I turned my phone back on, I realized that I'd received hundreds of texts overnight and my voice-mail inbox was full.

After listening to several "WTF?" messages from friends and colleagues, I couldn't deal with it anymore. I turned my phone off again, picked up the half-empty bottle of scotch and returned to my hiding spot on the couch.

I was woken up several hours later by someone pounding on my door. I lived on the eighth floor of a supposedly-secure apartment building, so I wondered who had managed to make it to my door. When I looked through the peep-hole, I could see RCMP Inspector Taylor's face staring back at me.

"Open up McKenzie, I know you're in there!"

I unlocked the door and pulled it open. "What do *you* want?"

He stared at me for several seconds. "You look like shit."

"Thanks, I feel like shit. So, as you can see, I'm not trying to hide anything from you. But unless you're here to arrest me, I've still got work to do on my latest project." I held up the bottle of scotch to show him how much progress I'd already made.

"I'm actually here as a friend to do a wellness check on you," he said. He took the bottle of scotch from my hand. "I also have some bad news."

"Great," I said. "My day has been nothing but sunshine and butterflies up until now."

He reached out and grabbed my shoulder. "Someone blew up Mary Byrnes' house last night."

Suddenly, every ounce of the scotch I had consumed over the last twenty-four hours came spewing out of my mouth.

CHAPTER 19

Taylor somehow managed to drag me back over to my couch where I collapsed.

"Mary is fine," he said. "She wasn't inside at the time, but the house was completely destroyed. The RCMP are still investigating whether it was intentional or an accident."

"I *know* it was intentional," I said. "Sarah Khan had threatened to kill her if we didn't stop looking for her."

"But now, *everyone* is looking for her," Taylor said. "Why would she escalate things even further? This whole case is now bigger than just exposing the secret that you and Powell faked her death. If she was smart, she'd just find someplace to lay low, not go around taking revenge on innocent people."

Taylor was right. Something about this didn't make sense. I slumped down on the couch.

"There's something else I discovered that doesn't add up," Taylor said.

"What's that?"

He reached over and pulled me toward him to make sure he had my full attention. "Nothing I'm about to tell you better appear in the newspaper, agreed?"

He seemed to forget that I didn't work for a newspaper anymore. "Agreed," I said.

"Superintendent Powell *did* file all of the necessary paperwork to get Sarah Khan admitted to the Witness Protection Program. It was approved by the highest levels within the government and the RCMP."

I had always assumed that to be true.

"But Powell never actually *put* her into the program," he added.

"I don't understand," I said.

"It's not easy to get someone into Witness Protection," Taylor said. "Powell's request was submitted to and approved by both the Crown Prosecutor and the Deputy Attorney General. At that point, all of the terms of the agreement are put in a Letter of Acknowledgement that must be signed by all of the parties involved, including the witness."

"What types of terms are we talking about?" I asked.

"It includes the obligations of both parties," Taylor said. "For the witness, they must agree to come back and testify at the appropriate time. They can't change their mind later on, or else they will be prosecuted themselves. For the government, it specifies where the witness will be relocated to, their new identity, and the financial obligations, typically how much money the government will pay them per month while they're in witness protection."

"Sounds reasonable," I said.

"Except Sarah Khan never signed the Letter of Acknowledgement."

"Could she have been put in the program without signing the letter?" I asked.

"Absolutely not," Taylor said. "Witnesses always seem

to assume they're going to be living a life of luxury while in the program, but in reality, it's usually a pretty basic lifestyle. That's why some witnesses decide it's not worth it and back out of the deal."

"So what would have happened to Sarah if she didn't agree to the terms?" I asked.

"Sarah wasn't totally innocent, even if you did believe it was her husband who poisoned all of those people on the plane," Taylor said. "We'd already charged her with multiple crimes, so she should have been prosecuted on those crimes and held in custody, even if only for her own protection."

"So what actually happened?" I asked.

"I don't know," Taylor said. "There's an internal investigation going on as we speak. The Witness Protection Program is completely separate from our main investigations department. If she'd been accepted, she would have been removed from Powell's authority and assigned to a new Witness Protection Officer who would be responsible for her. Even Powell wouldn't be able to reach her or even know her new ID or location."

"But that obviously didn't happen," I said.

"It appears not," Taylor said. "Those of us on the investigations side would have assumed she'd been moved into Witness Protection, and we're intentionally kept in the dark about where she is. But since the transfer was never actually completed, she should have still been under Powell's control in the investigations department."

"Something doesn't add up," I said.

"I agree," Taylor replied. "It appears that Powell signed her out as being transferred to Witness Protection, but she never actually made it there, and Powell's no longer around to tell us what really happened."

CHAPTER 20

The next morning, I decided to get on a plane to go see Mary in Newfoundland. Her life had been turned upside down due to my stupidity and I owed her an apology, face-to-face. However, I had no idea if she'd even agree to see me.

The first thing I did when I got to Gander was to head over to Mary's house, or more precisely, where her house used to be. Although that area of her street had been cordoned off, I could see there wasn't anything there except debris. Her neighbor's house to the north also had significant damage, although it was still standing. The property to the south was a construction site with only the foundation there. It looked like someone was in the midst of a tear-down and rebuild. There was an earth-digger laying on its side.

When I headed over to the hospital, I was told Mary was in the middle of her shift in the ICU and wouldn't be able to come out to talk to me for a few hours. Since I had nowhere else to go, I decided to wait for her in the hospital's cafeteria.

Mary came over to where I was sitting about two hours later.

"What are you doing here?" she asked. There was absolutely no warmth in her voice.

"I heard about the explosion and I wanted to make sure you were okay."

"Well, as you can see, I'm still alive, no thanks to you."

I suppose I deserved that. "I also wanted to apologize for getting you involved in all of this," I said. "I'm so, so sorry."

She just stared at me. "You still don't get it, do you?"

"Get what?"

"I'm not mad at you because a crazy person involved in one of your stories tried to kill me. I gladly went with you to Saudi Arabia to confront them and watch your back, knowing full well how dangerous some of those people could be. What I'm mad about..." Her voice started to tremble and I could tell she was about to cry. "What I'm so – *disappointed* about – is that you kept it all a secret from me. How can I ever trust you again?"

I could see the tears starting to form in her eyes and I couldn't bear to look at her. I hung my head in shame.

"I'm really, really sorry," I repeated, "and I'm also worried that you might still be in danger. Do you have someplace safe to stay? If you don't, you could come back to Toronto with me and stay at my place until things cool down."

I could tell by the look in her eyes that my suggestion was a non-starter. "I'm safe," she said. "I'm staying with a friend, someone who I can trust."

"Who's that?" I asked.

I heard a man's voice over my shoulder. "Dat would be me."

I recognized the thick Newfie accent and turned to see

Inspector Pat Murphy standing there. Murphy was the local RCMP officer who had first interviewed me when I'd been taken off the plane where almost every other passenger had died. He was a good guy and a good cop, but he'd been pulled off of the investigation when the senior RCMP officers from Ottawa had taken over the case.

I reached out to shake his hand. "Inspector Murphy, it's been a while."

"Sure has," he said. "When Mary's house blew up, I was de first copper on de scene. T'ank God she wasn't home at the time."

"That was just luck," Mary said. "I was supposed to be at home, but I'd been called back into the ICU because of a car accident. There were several people injured and they needed all hands on deck."

"So, have you been assigned to keep Mary safe?" I asked Inspector Murphy.

I noticed that he and Mary shared a look.

"Since my house blew up and I didn't have any other place to stay," Mary said, "Pat, here, said I could stay at his place while they completed their investigation. He has a big house with a spare bedroom."

I had noticed that Mary had referred to him as *Pat* and not as *Inspector Murphy*. I suspected that Murphy hadn't made the offer to let Mary stay at his place in a strictly official capacity. I remembered my impression from a year earlier that he had a bit of thing for Mary.

"Here on the rock, we help each ot'er out, whene'er we can," Murphy said.

In a way, I was glad that Mary was staying with him. She probably couldn't get much safer than staying with an RCMP officer. Still, I could feel the pull on my heartstrings.

"Are you ready to go?" Murphy asked Mary.

"I just have to run upstairs to get something," she said.

After she left, there was an awkward silence between Murphy and myself. By default, I slipped back into investigative journalist mode.

"How's your investigation into the explosion going?" I asked. "Any leads on where Sarah Khan might be hiding?"

"De investigation is still goin' on," Murphy said, "but we actually t'ink it might have just been an accident. It appears that the guy buildin' de house next to Mary's might'a broken a gas line when he was doing some landscaping. He didna' realize it cuz it was just a slow leak, but we t'ink dat the gas just built up 'til she finally blew. We're lucky no one was around at the time and no one got hurt."

"So you don't think Sarah Khan is behind the explosion?" I asked. "Did Mary tell you about the threats she made?"

"Yeah, Mary told us everyt'ing. But we don't t'ink Sarah Khan is involved at all."

Mary returned a few seconds later. "I'm ready to go," she said to Murphy.

As I watched them walk out of the hospital, I had the distinct impression that Mary was walking out of my life forever.

"Take care," I shouted after them.

She didn't look back.

CHAPTER 21

A few days after I got home from my trip to Gander, there was a knock on my apartment door. Once again, our so-called top-notch security system in the building had failed to do its job. I peered through the peep-hole to see Dawood Khan standing outside in the hallway, along with his personal bodyguard, Majeed.

"Gentlemen," I said as I opened the door. "What brings you to my door?"

"We've already stopped by a few times over the last few days, but you weren't home," Dawood said. "We were wondering if you've made any progress tracking down Sarah."

I invited them into my living room. "I was in Newfoundland for a few days," I said. "Someone blew up my girlfriend's house and I thought Sarah might have been behind it, but the police think it was just an accident."

"I agree," Dawood said. "Sarah is a lot of things, but she's not a person who would murder an innocent bystander."

I noticed Majeed was doing a sweep of my apartment

making sure there was no one else present.

"Can I get you guys anything?" I asked. "Coffee, tea?" I realized I had no idea what people from Saudi Arabia drank in the morning.

"We're good," Dawood said.

Majeed didn't even acknowledge that I'd asked him a question.

"I see from the press that the secret about you and that cop putting Sarah into the Witness Protection Program has now become public knowledge," Dawood said. "I'm sorry to hear you lost your job over it, but I guess that was to be expected."

He didn't seem sorry at all.

"I've now discovered that although the authorities *approved* Sarah's admission into the program, she never actually made it *into* the program," I said.

"Yes, we've discovered that as well," Dawood said.

It appeared that he had good sources of information, which didn't surprise me at all.

"To answer your original question," I said, "I have no idea where Sarah is right now. But I have a question for you…"

Dawood nodded for me to proceed.

"What do you intend to do if you do find her?" I asked.

"I plan to take her back to Saudi Arabia," he said, "for her own protection. She is, even after everything she's done, still my wife."

"Do you think she's in danger?" I asked.

"Absolutely," he said. "If your authorities find her first, I'm sure they'll put her in jail. But if my brother finds her before they do, I'm not sure she'll be that lucky. That's why it's important that I find her before he does." He paused for a second. "But that begs the question, what will *you* do if you find her?"

"I have no idea," I said, which was the absolute truth. But then I thought about it a little more. "I guess I'd turn her into the police and let the courts decide her fate. But, since I no longer have a job, I'm not sure I have the resources to keep looking for her."

Dawood smiled. "If you help me find her before either my brother or the police do, I would be glad to compensate you for your time."

The idea intrigued me, but I wasn't sure I wanted to get into a partnership with Dawood. "I'm not sure I'm even going to look for her anymore," I said.

Dawood studied me. "Don't lie to me," he said, "or to yourself. You know as well as I do that you can't just let this drop."

After Dawood and his bodyguard left, I thought about what Dawood had said and realized he was right. There was no way I was going to stop looking for Sarah.

However, I had no idea how to find her. I decided to follow one of the guiding principles of all journalists – follow the money.

Dawood had told me when I was in Saudi Arabia that Sarah had moved $100 million Saudi Riyal (about $36 million Canadian Dollars) into hidden offshore accounts. While I knew there was no way she was actually walking around with that kind of money in her back pocket, I figured she'd need access to some cash just to get around.

I called up an old contact who worked at one of the government organizations that investigated suspected money laundering cases. We'd known each other for over twenty years and he had helped me in the past. I told him what I was looking for, but this time, he seemed reluctant to help me. It appeared that being exposed about fabricating someone's death in the newspaper closes a lot of doors.

"Okay, let's just do a hypothetical," I said. "If I had a shitload of money sitting in offshore accounts, how could I get some of that money into Canada so I could use it?"

"How much money are we talking about," he asked, "hypothetically?"

"About thirty-six million in total," I said, "but I'd probably keep most of it hidden away. I'd only need to pull in enough to keep me living in the style to which I've become accustomed."

"Well, since I know you like to live pretty high on the hog, I'd suggest you find yourself a shady investment company that would help you bring the money into Canada in small chunks, keeping each transaction under the ten thousand dollar limit so it doesn't have to be reported."

"How would I find one of these shady investment companies?" I asked. "Are there a lot of them to choose from?"

"You'd be surprised," he said, "but they don't tend to advertise exactly what they do. You'd have to know someone who knows someone who knows someone."

"What if I was new in town?" I asked, "and haven't established any contacts yet. How would I find one in that case?"

"That makes it harder," he said. "In that situation, you'd probably need a recommendation from the other end."

"What do you mean?"

"If the money is currently being held in one or more offshore accounts, then whoever is currently holding that money will probably have someone they prefer to work with in each country. Is the person you're trying to find in a major center like Toronto, Vancouver or Montreal?"

"I'm not really sure," I said, "but if I had to guess, I think they're probably somewhere in interior BC. Does that make it harder?"

"No, that might actually make it easier," he said. "Most of the shady investment firms are in the bigger cities, so you'd have fewer companies to investigate in a smaller place."

"So how do I find out which one she's using?" I asked.

"You mean this hypothetical person we're talking about?"

"Yes."

"I can't tell you that," he said. "All I can give you is background info to narrow down your search. After that, it's up to you to do the legwork."

When I hung up the phone, I didn't feel like I was any further ahead. But I was surprised when he called me again a few days later. "You didn't hear this from me," he said.

"Agreed."

"I have no idea if this will help you at all, but there's a small investment firm in Vernon that fits the profile of the hypothetical company we were talking about. It's a company we've had on our watch-list for quite a while now for doing some shady real estate investments with offshore money."

"Great," I said. "What's the name of the company?"

"You know I can't tell you that," he said, "but if I were looking for this hypothetical person, I'd be focusing on the Vernon area."

"Thanks," I said. "How would this person actually get the cash once the funds are transferred to the investment firm, hypothetically speaking?"

"There are a few ways," he said, "but I've often seen

them use a cheque made out to a shell company with the person set up as an officer of the company, sometimes using a fake name. They're always coming up with new ways to muddy the trail."

I thanked him for the tip. Maybe all of my old contacts weren't totally dead after all. At least I now had a destination – Vernon.

I remembered travelling through Vernon when I'd driven from Kelowna to Enderby to see Kathleen Powell. I'd suspected that Sarah had been involved in the apparent suicide of Superintendent Powell, even though all evidence had indicated otherwise. I figured that returning to British Columbia was my best chance of finding Sarah.

CHAPTER 22

I flew out to Kelowna a few days later and made the short drive to Vernon. Since my source hadn't told me the name of the investment company involved in these suspicious transactions, I decided to google investment firms located in the area. There were more than I thought.

I narrowed down the list by removing all of the firms associated with the big Canadian institutions, figuring there would be less of a chance they'd be involved. To my surprise, there were still a lot of companies left on the list for a relatively small community.

A few seemed to specialize in real estate investments, particularly from China. I recalled an article in the newspaper from several months earlier about a Chinese man who had an income of about forty thousand dollars a year who had purchased over thirty-two million dollars of real estate in BC by transferring money from offshore accounts. I was sure Sarah would be working with an investment company who worked with individuals like him.

I refined my search even further by looking for firms who had very few online reviews. Companies who provided questionable services for people looking to hide or launder money usually wanted to fly under the radar and weren't looking for glowing five-star reviews. That narrowed my search to a handful of companies.

I visited each of the companies to get an initial assessment, but four out of the five were closed, even though it was the middle of the day. I suspected very few meetings with clients ever happened in these offices and wondered if they were just being used as mail-drops.

The fifth company had a young, bored girl sitting behind the desk playing games on her computer. She barely looked old enough to be out of high school. In our brief conversation, I determined that the owner of the company was her grandfather who was a semi-retired financial planner. He only had a few rich, older clients who he still looked after, and he'd hired his grand-daughter to work as his receptionist. This was not the type of company that Sarah would be dealing with.

I stopped by the other four companies several times over the next few days, but never found them open. I called the telephone numbers shown on their doors and left voice-mails, but never got a return call.

Now that I was no longer on the newspaper's payroll and expense account, I could not afford to stay in hotel rooms in Vernon for any extended length of time waiting to pick up a lead on Sarah's location. But I decided to give it just a few more days.

I camped out at each of the four investment company offices for a few hours each day, hoping that someone would show up. I even visited them during the evenings, thinking that their clients might prefer off-hour meetings, but still got nowhere.

It was when I was driving around Vernon one evening visiting each of these investment companies that I had the sense that someone was following me. I made a few unnecessary turns and sure enough, my tail made the same turns. He was a pretty good tail because he was staying well-back, too far back for me to discern who it might be.

When I drove back to my motel that night, I noticed that my tail parked down the street, far enough away not to be obvious, but close enough to track my movements.

Since my budget was limited, I wasn't staying at a first-class hotel. I was staying at the type of motel where you parked your car right outside your room. It wasn't fancy, but it was clean, which is why I'd chosen it.

With my car still parked out front, I removed the screen and climbed out the window in the back of my room. Then I made a wide circle to come up from behind whoever was tailing me.

I noted the license plate number of the vehicle, but then realized it would be useless when I saw the "Budget" rental car sticker on the bumper.

There were a couple of teenagers walking down the sidewalk and I fell in behind them as we approached the car from the rear. As I walked by the car, I looked in the passenger-side window and immediately recognized the person. It was Dawood Khan's bodyguard, Majeed.

I tapped on the window and waved for him to unlock the door. He seemed embarrassed to have been caught, but did as I requested.

"How long have you been following me?" I asked.

"Ever since you flew out to Kelowna," he said. "I'm surprised it took you this long to spot me."

"Is your boss close by?"

"He's staying at a hotel a couple of kilometers from

here."

I was sure it would be a higher class hotel than the one I was staying in.

Majeed looked at his watch. "I'm supposed to check in with him about now. Do you want to talk to him?"

I nodded my agreement and Majeed called him using his cell phone. They spoke briefly to each other in Arabic and then Majeed handed the phone to me.

"Do you think following me around is the best way for you to track down Sarah?" I asked.

"It's not the only method I'm using," he said, "but I thought I'd have Majeed keep tabs on you just in case you found her first. You really should have partnered up with me, you know. I would have paid for you to stay in a better hotel than that dump you're currently holed up in."

"Well you might as well give Majeed the rest of the night off," I said, "because I'm checking out of my motel first thing tomorrow morning and flying back to Toronto. I haven't found any trace of Sarah."

"Yes, I know," Dawood said. "I was hoping you'd be more successful."

"Should I expect to see the two of you on the same flight tomorrow?" I asked. "It will be easier for you to tail me if you're sitting in the seat behind me."

"I'm not sure if we'll be on the same flight or not," Dawood said, "but we won't be in the seats behind you. We're accustomed to flying first-class. My offer to become partners in the search for Sarah still stands. If you accept, you'd be able to fly first-class as well."

"Thanks, but no thanks," I said.

I hung up the phone and handed it to Majeed. "I'm just walking back to my motel right now if you want to take the rest of the night off," I said as I got out of the car. "I won't be going anywhere until the morning, but I will be having a pizza delivered to my room if you're interested in joining me."

He smiled. "Thank you for the offer, sir, but I'm not a fan of pizza. Have a pleasant evening."

He watched me cross the street and back over to my motel room. When the pizza guy showed up about forty-five minutes later, I could still see Majeed sitting in the car watching me.

CHAPTER 23

My cell phone rang the next morning before the sun was up.

"Are you still looking for Sarah Khan?" a woman's voice asked.

I recognized the voice, but couldn't put a face to it, possibly because I was still half asleep.

"Yes I am," I said. "Who *is* this?"

"Kathleen Powell. I figured you'd still be looking for her."

I was still a little groggy. "Do you think you know where she is?" I asked.

"I know *exactly* where she is," she said, "because I'm looking right at her as we speak."

Suddenly, I was wide awake. "Where are you?" I asked.

"I'm at the Vancouver airport. Sarah is about to board a flight to Trinidad and Tobago. And I'm about to board the same flight."

"Are sure it's her?" I asked.

"She's changed how she looks," Kathleen said, "but I

know it's her. She's cut her hair quite short and changed the color. It's actually purple on one side."

That sounded totally bizarre to me. "Why would she be going to Trinidad?" I asked, "and why are you following her?"

"I have no idea why she's going to Trinidad," Kathleen said, "and I don't care. I'm following her because I'm convinced she murdered my husband and I'm going to make her pay for that – with her life."

"Kathleen, don't do anything stupid. I'll get on the next flight to Trinidad and we can figure this all out. Promise me you won't do anything until I can get there."

"I'm not making any promises," she said. "Gotta go, our flight is boarding."

And then she hung up.

I jumped out of bed, grabbed a quick shower and threw my clothes into my suitcase. I also googled flights to Trinidad and discovered there were very few. My best bet was to fly from Kelowna to Vancouver, then on to Houston, and then finally to Trinidad.

When I stepped out of my room in Vernon, I could see Majeed's rental car still parked down the street. He followed me as I drove from Vernon to the Kelowna airport. Since I didn't want Dawood and his bodyguard knowing where I was headed next, I had to come up with a plan to lose them.

Sure enough, I could see Majeed watching me as I checked in at the counter at the airport, supposedly for my flight from Kelowna back to Toronto. I hoped he wasn't paying close enough attention to realize that I had switched my flight to fly to Vancouver instead. As an investigative journalist, I always had to be prepared to fly anywhere at any time, so I always had my passport with me to accommodate any last minute changes in plans.

When I entered the security line at the airport, I saw Majeed leave the airport to head back to Vernon to pick up his boss. It appeared my deception had worked.

CHAPTER 24

It seemed to take me forever to get to Trinidad. I had to do an overnight layover in Houston before catching the flight to Trinidad the following morning. I used the opportunity to purchase some new clothes in Houston because I hadn't packed suitable clothing for a trip to Trinidad. I was pleased that my credit card wasn't rejected, because I knew I was getting pretty close to my limit. Purchasing a last minute airline ticket to fly to Trinidad had been pricey.

Even though I was exhausted, I called Kathleen as soon as I landed. She had arrived at least a day before me and I prayed she hadn't done anything stupid in the meantime. I was pleased when she answered, because I had just called the last number she had called me from in Canada, and I wasn't sure it would connect.

"Kathleen, it's Andrew McKenzie. I've just landed in Trinidad. Where are you?"

She gave me the name of her hotel and I told the taxi driver to take me there, which fortunately, was quite close to the airport.

"You took your time getting here," Kathleen said when she opened the door.

"I got here as fast as I could," I said. "I had a layover in Houston."

She offered me a cold drink with some ice, which I gratefully accepted. "So, where's Sarah?" I asked.

"She's staying at a hotel not far from here," she said, "a much nicer hotel, I might add."

"And you're sure it's Sarah?"

"Positive."

She pulled out her cell phone and showed me a picture that she'd taken of Sarah at the Vancouver airport. I zoomed in on the photo and confirmed that it was Sarah.

"Have you figured out what she's doing here?" I asked.

"She's been meeting with a bunch of people," she said.

"Who?"

"I haven't figured that out yet, but I took pictures of some of them."

Kathleen swiped a few times on her phone and then handed it to me. The first picture was of a group of people taken in the lobby of a hotel. I had no idea who any of them were.

"If you keep scrolling, I took a few more individual shots," she said.

I scrolled through a few and then stopped on the fourth. "Holy shit!"

"Did you recognize someone?" Kathleen asked.

"Yes," I said. "He's a former FIFA executive. He's one of the people the U.S. Justice Department charged with wire fraud, racketeering and money laundering."

"Then why isn't he in jail?" Kathleen asked.

"Because he's fighting the extradition to the United States. Some people think he'll die of old age before he ever spends a day in jail."

"Why do you think he's meeting with Sarah?" Kathleen asked.

"I don't know," I said, "but I suspect that it has something to do with Sarah's shady deals in getting the construction contracts for the World Cup held in Qatar."

"But that's over and done with," Kathleen said. "Why would she be meeting with him now?"

"Perhaps this was the payoff meeting," I said. "Sarah moved a ton of money into offshore accounts before she fled from Qatar. There's a lot of people looking for her right now. By the way, how did *you* manage to find her?"

"Don't you remember what I told you when we last met?" Kathleen said.

I thought back to when we'd talked about her husband's apparent suicide. "You told me you resigned from the RCMP when you married Simon and went into intelligence work, but you didn't say who you worked for."

Kathleen smiled. "I told you that was on a need-to-know basis and that you didn't need to know."

"And what about now?"

"You *still* don't need to know. Let's just say I found Sarah by following the money."

"That's what I did as well," I said. "That led me to a few investment companies in Vernon, but I didn't get any further than that."

"Let's just say I have access to a few more resources than you do," Kathleen said.

"Where is Sarah now?" I asked.

"She's back at her hotel, probably packing." Kathleen looked at her watch. "The meetings appear to be over, and Sarah is booked on a flight back to Canada in about four and a half hours. I know, because I'm booked on the same flight."

"Aren't you worried that she'll recognize you?"

"She has no idea what I look like," Kathleen said, "and even if she did, I'll make a few subtle changes to how I look before I get on the flight."

"Fuck!" I said. "I got here just in time to turn around and leave again."

"You can't come on the same flight," Kathleen said. "You've met with her numerous times. She'd spot you in an instant."

I knew she was right.

"Besides," she said. "You look exhausted. Why don't you just stay here overnight and fly back tomorrow? I've already paid for the room until tomorrow anyway."

"You're not going to do anything to hurt Sarah, are you?" I asked.

"I won't do anything to her until I find out, for sure, whether she murdered my husband. Once I do that, I'm not going to make any promises."

Kathleen left for the airport a few hours later. Before she left, she transferred the pictures she'd taken from her phone to my phone. I spent the evening trying to identify any of the other people attending the meetings with Sarah and the former FIFA executive. I wasn't having much luck.

I looked back to the group photo she'd taken in the hotel lobby and noticed someone standing in the background. I zoomed in on the photo and recognized Ahmad Khan's bodyguard. And if his bodyguard was in that hotel lobby, I knew that Ahmad wouldn't be far away.

CHAPTER 25

I called Dawood as soon as I landed back in Canada. He'd left me a few voice-mails which I'd picked up while in Trinidad, but I'd been putting off calling him back. He was quite pissed that I'd managed to evade the tail he'd put on me.

"Where the hell have you been?" he said as soon as he answered, "and have you found Sarah?"

"I was in Trinidad," I said. "Sarah was there meeting with a former FIFA executive and a bunch of other people I haven't identified yet."

"Is she still there?" Dawood asked.

"No, she flew back to Vancouver. I don't know where she is now, but I suspect that she's still somewhere in British Columbia."

"How did you find her?" he asked.

I didn't want to tell him that Kathleen Powell was actually the person who had found her. "That's not important," I said, "but what is, is that I think your brother is hot on Sarah's trail."

"Was he there in Trinidad?" he asked.

"I didn't see him, but I know his bodyguard was there, so Ahmad was probably there as well."

Dawood said something in Arabic that I didn't understand.

"You should probably know that Sarah has changed her appearance," I added. "She's now sporting short blonde hair with purple streaks on the side."

Dawood said something else in Arabic. That's when I realized that he wasn't talking to me, but to someone else in the room with him, probably to Majeed, his bodyguard.

"Where are you now?" Dawood asked me.

"I'm in Vancouver, but I'm planning to head back to Vernon. I think that Sarah is hiding out somewhere in interior BC."

"Majeed is booking a flight for us to come out there as we speak. Will you be staying in the same flea-bag motel that you were staying at before?"

"Probably," I said.

"You know, if you just agreed to partner up with me, I'd cover all of your expenses and you'd be able to stay in a much nicer place."

His offer was tempting, but not quite tempting enough. "Thanks, but no thanks," I said.

Once I got off the phone with Dawood, I called Inspector Taylor. I didn't get to speak to him, but left him a voice-mail giving him the latest updates, including my trip to Trinidad.

I figured the best outcome would be if the RCMP could find Sarah and arrest her. If Dawood found her first, he would probably sneak her out of the country and back to Saudi Arabia. Since Canada and Saudi Arabia don't have an extradition agreement, we'd never be able to bring her to justice.

If Ahmad found her first, he'd probably kill her after

getting her to reveal where she'd hidden all of the money she'd stolen from their construction company.

But I was also worried about Kathleen Powell. She'd made it clear that she'd also kill Sarah if she found out, for sure, that Sarah had killed her husband and faked his suicide.

Inspector Taylor called me back a few hours later.

"Where are you now?" he asked me.

"I'm at the Kelowna airport," I said. "I'm just about to rent a car and drive to Vernon."

"Is that where Sarah is?"

"I don't know," I said, "but I think she's somewhere in the area."

"I've already alerted the RCMP detachments in BC to be on the lookout for her," Taylor said.

"She's changed her appearance," I told him. I told him I'd text him a picture of her from my phone. He confirmed he'd received it a few seconds later.

"I'm also going to send you a picture of some of the people she was meeting with in Trinidad. The only one I know is a former FIFA executive who's already been charged by the U.S. Justice Department with wire fraud and corruption. Maybe the RCMP can figure out who the other people are."

"Got it," Taylor said.

"How did Sarah manage to get out of, and then back into Canada on an international flight?" I asked. "Didn't you have her on some kind of no-fly list?"

"We do," Taylor said. "We've got her on the list under three names, Sarah Brooks, Sarah Khan, and Sarah Brooks Khan, but her fake passport used a different name."

"What name is she using now?" I asked.

"She's going by Sarah McKenzie," Taylor said.

I was stunned. "She's using *my* last name?"

"I told you she liked you," Taylor said. I could almost see him grinning through the phone.

After ending my call with Inspector Taylor, I drove from the Kelowna airport to Vernon and checked into the motel in the early evening. Then I called Kathleen Powell.

"I'm back in Canada," I told her. "Do you know where Sarah is?"

"Yes," Kathleen said. "I'm sitting in my car on a little side road watching her through binoculars right now. She's staying in a rented house out in the middle of nowhere. She's not alone and they seem pretty settled in, as if they're waiting for someone else to arrive."

"Who's she with?" I asked.

"I haven't figured that out yet. If she was alone, Sarah and I would have already had our one-on-one conversation about what she did to my husband."

"Where are you?"

"Why do you need to know?" she asked. "What are you planning to do?"

"Look, I'm just trying to get Sarah into custody without anyone getting killed," I said.

"Don't bullshit me," Kathleen said. "You're looking to get the story. The number one goal of all journalists is *always* to get the story before anyone else. You don't give a shit about who gets hurt in the process."

"That's not true," I said. "There are a few things you should know. First, all of the RCMP detachments in BC are on the lookout for Sarah. If they find her, they will arrest her."

"If that was the case, why didn't they just arrest her at the Vancouver airport?"

"Because she circumvented their no-fly list by using a

fake passport and a fake name. She's now using the name of Sarah McKenzie."

"You've got to be kidding me."

"I wish I was", I said. "Second, Sarah's husband, Dawood, is on his way to BC right now. If he finds her, I think he'll try to sneak her out of the country and back to Saudi Arabia where she'll be able to avoid prosecution."

"Maybe that's who she's waiting for?" Kathleen said.

"I don't think so," I said. "Dawood doesn't even know where she is. He's trying to get me to partner up with him to help find her."

"And are you helping him?"

"Not really," I said.

"That's a non-answer answer. Are you helping him or not?"

"Like I said before, I'm hoping the police arrest her and bring her to justice, without anyone else getting killed. And that's the third thing I wanted to tell you. Dawood's brother, Ahmad, is also looking for Sarah and he is one scary son-of-a-bitch. Sarah stole a lot of money from them and hid it in offshore accounts. I'm pretty sure he followed her to Trinidad, so he probably also followed her back to Canada. If he finds her first, I'm pretty sure he'll kill her."

"What does this guy look like?" Kathleen asked. "Maybe that's who's with her right now."

"I'll send his picture to your phone. You've already got a picture of his bodyguard because he was in the background of the group photo you took in Trinidad."

"Got it," Kathleen said about a minute later. "You're right, he looks mean, but he's not the guy in the house with Sarah right now." There was a pause of several seconds. "I'm looking at the group photo right now. Which one is the bodyguard?"

"He's the one in the back-left of the group photo. He's half hidden by the pillar in the lobby, but if you zoom in, you'll be able to see his face."

"Hold on a second," Kathleen said. "That's the same guy that's with Sarah right now," she said a few seconds later. "I just confirmed it's him by looking at him through the binoculars."

"Does it look like he's holding Sarah hostage?" I asked.

"No, they look like two friends just sitting around waiting for someone else to arrive," Kathleen said.

Nothing happened for a few minutes.

"A car just drove up to the house," Kathleen said, "but I can't see who's in it."

I listened impatiently, waiting for Kathleen to tell me what was happening, but all I could hear was her breathing.

"Sweet Jesus!" she gasped.

"What's going on?" I asked. "Who was in the car that just drove up?"

"The scary dude and it looks like some shit is about to do down."

"Kathleen," I yelled into my phone. "Where are you? I'll send help."

"I don't know the exact address, but it's an old farmhouse south of Salmon Arm, a few miles north of highway 97. Gotta go."

"Kathleen, I think you should wait for help to arrive."

But my advice fell upon deaf ears. She'd already hung up.

CHAPTER 26

I immediately called 9-1-1 and told the dispatcher what was happening. However, since I didn't have an exact address to give them, all I got was a commitment to dispatch a car to the general area to investigate.

Frustrated, I called Inspector Taylor who answered immediately, even though it was close to midnight, Ottawa time. I told him what was happening and he said he'd escalate the call and provide instructions to the officers out at the local detachment.

I sat in my motel room in Vernon for a few minutes waiting for any updates, but then decided to drive to the area that Kathleen had described. If something was happening, I figured I'd just follow the flashing lights of the police cars to the scene. But there was nothing.

I drove up and down Salmon River Road a few times, but didn't see anything out of the ordinary. I also drove up and down a few of the other roads in the area, but got the same result. I tried calling Kathleen Powell, but got no answer. I tried calling Inspector Taylor, but he didn't answer this time either. Frustrated by not knowing what was going on, I parked my rental car outside of the Silver Creek Volunteer Fire Department building and waited for someone, anyone, to tell me what was happening.

I only saw one RCMP cruiser when I was driving around and he didn't seem to be in a hurry to get anywhere, just out on a regular patrol.

Finally, just after two in the morning, I got a call from Kathleen. "You should come up to the hiking trail near my place in Enderby," she said.

"Which hiking trail?" I asked.

"The one where Simon was killed," she said, "and come alone."

"What's happened?" I asked, but she had already hung up.

I drove my rental car to Kathleen's place which took me longer than I thought it would. Everything looked different at night.

I stopped at a few gas stations in Salmon Arm hoping to be able to buy a flashlight, but they were all closed at this time of night. Fortunately, I found a small convenience store that was still open, and purchased one.

As I started up the hiking trail near Kathleen's house, I discovered that it was a pretty crappy flashlight. I was worried that I'd make a misstep and fall to my death over one of the cliffs.

As I waved the flashlight from side to side, the beam picked up a flash of bright yellow. When I took a closer look, I saw that it was crime-scene tape. Although most of the tape surrounding the area where Superintendent Powell's apparent suicide had taken place had been removed long ago, there were still a few strands dangling from the branches of the surrounding trees. I peered over the ledge of the cliff and could see more crime-scene tape down below. That was probably where they'd found his body. I had an eerie feeling.

"Over here," I heard Kathleen yell out.

I turned toward the sound and saw the beam of Kathleen's flashlight a little farther up the trail. As I approached, I saw Kathleen holding a gun pointed directly at Sarah. Sarah was shivering, either from fright, or the cold, or both. Kathleen seemed totally calm.

"Where's Ahmad and his bodyguard?" I asked.

"They're both dead," Kathleen said. "It appears that Sarah here pulled another double-cross. She was working in cahoots with the bodyguard. They lured Ahmad to that little house in the country by having his bodyguard say that he'd found Sarah, and the bodyguard killed Ahmad as soon as he arrived."

"So what happened to the bodyguard?" I asked.

"Sarah shot him," Kathleen said, "didn't you?"

I looked at Sarah, but she just stared at the ground.

"Tell him!" Kathleen shouted.

"Yes," Sarah said softly.

"I saw the whole thing happen before my eyes," Kathleen said. "She's just a cold-blooded killer who murders anyone who gets in her way. When Ahmad's bodyguard tracked her down, she said she'd split all of the money she'd stolen with him if he killed his boss. And when he did, she pulled another double-cross and killed the bodyguard, so *now* she doesn't have to share the money with anyone."

"Is that true?" I asked Sarah.

She nodded her agreement.

"So, turn her into the police," I said to Kathleen. "She'll be charged and go to prison."

"Prison is too good for her," Kathleen said.

"So, why am I here, Kathleen?" I asked. "Why did you invite me up here in the middle of the night?"

She seemed surprised by the question. "You wanted the story and I'm giving you the story, but we're not done yet." She turned toward Sarah. "Tell him how you murdered my husband."

Sarah raised her head and pleaded with me. "I didn't kill him, I swear. I'll tell you everything but please, please don't let her kill me."

"Tell him!" Kathleen screamed.

"Simon said he'd put me into the witness protection program," Sarah said, "but when he came back with the agreement for me to sign, I found out that I'd be living out here in the middle of nowhere and expected to live on practically nothing. I'd have to give up all of that money that I'd stashed away in the offshore accounts."

She started to cry as she continued telling what had happened. "So I offered Simon half of the money if he just let me walk away – and he agreed."

"He would *never* do that," Kathleen said.

"I swear, he did," Sarah pleaded. "He found a place for me to live out here in BC and I started pulling the money out of the offshore accounts in small amounts. Every time I pulled some money out, I sent him half."

"I don't believe you!" Kathleen said.

"It's true," Sarah said. "But shortly after you moved out here, Simon started to feel guilty about what we'd done. He said he was going to come clean and turn himself in to the police. When we met up here the morning he died, I tried to talk him out of it, but he said the guilt was killing him."

"So you killed him," Kathleen said.

"No, I didn't," Sarah said. She turned toward Kathleen. "I did threaten to do something to you if he turned me in or helped the police track me down, but I never actually would have done anything to hurt you. It was just a threat."

"Just like you threatened to harm Mary if I didn't stop looking for you," I said.

"Exactly," Sarah said, "but I never would have actually hurt her. I'm not a monster. I had nothing to do with that explosion at her house. You have to believe me."

I'm not sure why, but I believed what Sarah was telling us. But then again, she'd already fooled me so many times that I questioned my ability to detect a lie from the truth.

There was a silence for a long time.

"You should leave us now," Kathleen said to me.

"What are you going to do?" I asked.

"Just leave," she said.

"If you do something stupid, I can't promise not to tell the police what happened here today," I said.

"I'm not asking you to," Kathleen said. "It's up to you to decide what you keep secret. You can tell the police if you want, or tell the whole fucking world if you want. I don't care. But you should definitely leave and not look back."

As I walked away down the path toward my car, I wondered what Kathleen was going to do. I had almost reached my car when the cheap flashlight I'd purchased gave out and I was thrust into total darkness.

That's when I heard the single gunshot. The sound echoed through the surrounding mountains.

I thought about running back up the path, but then decided against it. I used the light from my cell phone to navigate the final few yards toward my car. Then I got in the car and drove to the motel in Vernon. When I got to my room, I turned off my phone and crawled into bed, pulling the covers over my head. I had to escape from the world, even if it was only for a few hours.

CHAPTER 27

When I woke up the next morning and turned my phone back on, it beeped to tell me that I'd missed numerous calls. Several were from a local police officer, another was from Inspector Taylor and the last one was from Dawood Khan. I called Inspector Taylor first.

"Where the hell *are* you?" he asked.

"I'm in a motel room in Vernon," I said. "I turned off my phone overnight to escape from the world for a few hours. Where are you?"

"I'm at a crime scene out on Yankee Flats Road, just south of Salmon Arm. I caught the first flight out after you called me last night saying something was going down. You were right. I'm looking at two dead bodies that were discovered here a few hours ago."

I remembered driving up and down Yankee Flats Road the previous night, so I knew the general area. "Give me the exact address and I'll come to you," I said.

When I got there, the place was crawling with cops and reporters. The area had been cordoned off with crime scene tape. I told the cop guarding the scene who I was and he called Inspector Taylor on his radio. Taylor walked up to me a few minutes later.

"We've got two dead bodies in the house," he said, "both shot at point-blank range."

"I know," I said. "It's Ahmad Khan and his bodyguard."

"How do you know that?" he asked. "Were you here?"

"No," I said. I nodded toward his car. "Let's talk in private and I'll tell you everything I know."

When we got inside the cruiser, I told him what Kathleen Powell had told me the previous night, about how the bodyguard had shot Ahmad, and then how Sarah had shot the bodyguard.

"I think I might know where you'll find another body," I said.

Following my directions, Inspector Taylor and I drove to Kathleen Powell's house in the cruiser. I half expected to see Kathleen sitting on her deck waiting for us to arrive, but the place looked deserted.

"Follow me," I said to Taylor.

I led him up the trail to where Kathleen, Sarah and I had talked the night before. As we walked, I told him about the conversation we'd had, about how Sarah and Superintendent Powell had worked out a deal to make her disappear, but then how he'd changed his mind and then killed himself out of guilt, and to protect his wife.

When we got to the exact meeting spot, I expected to see Sarah lying on the ground in a pool of blood, but there was nothing there. Inspector Taylor radioed it in and the police searched the entire area, but they didn't find any bodies or any evidence of foul play.

Two people had completely vanished without a trace, Kathleen Powell and Sarah Khan.

The next day, Dawood confronted me and asked me if I knew where his wife was. I told him the truth. I had no idea.

For some reason, I never told anyone about the single gunshot I'd heard that night just before I'd reached my car. I had assumed that Kathleen had killed Sarah, but maybe I was wrong. If she had, I wouldn't have blamed her. Was I withholding that information to protect Kathleen?

This whole mess had started because I had kept a secret, thinking I was doing the right thing, but it had come back to haunt me. And yet here I was, doing it again.

Some people never learn.

THE END

Watch for the next book in the Andrew McKenzie series, expected to be released in 2025.

OTHER BOOKS BY

E.A. BRIGINSHAW

Goliath

Henry Shaw leads a relatively quiet life trying to balance his work at a growing law firm with his family life, including supporting his teenage son who has a promising soccer career ahead of him. But all of that changes when Henry's bipolar brother, in one of his manic states, tells him that Goliath didn't really die as told in the biblical story – and that he is Goliath.

When his brother disappears along with a media magnate, the FBI and the local police believe they may have been part of a secret international network and that Goliath was his brother's code name. The solution to this puzzle may reside in his brother's laptop computer, which mysteriously disappears during a break-in at his house.

Is his brother dead or just hiding from forces trying to destroy the network? Henry tries to solve the puzzle along with an intriguing woman he encounters at an airport bar.

Book (ISBN 978-0-9921390-0-1)
eBook (ISBN 978-0-9921390-1-8)

The Second Shooter

It has been widely speculated that the FBI, CIA and Secret Service have been hiding the existence of critical evidence as to those involved in the assassination of President John F. Kennedy. The JFK Records Act requires that all records related to the assassination be released to the public by October 26, 2017, unless the President deems their release would cause grave harm to the nation. When some of these potentially dangerous records are accidentally released, forces within the government attempt to recover them using whatever means necessary, including the elimination of anyone who may have seen them.

In the sequel to "Goliath", David and Robert Shaw head off to university and find themselves drawn into the world of shadow governments and secret societies. Despite the work of an investigative journalist to uncover the truth, and the efforts of their father to protect them, they find themselves squarely in the crosshairs of "The Second Shooter".

Book   (ISBN 978-0-9921390-4-9)
eBook (ISBN 978-0-9921390-5-6)

The Third Option

Henry Shaw is faced with a very difficult decision. The FBI have claimed that his son, David, has been radicalized and become part of a terrorist group involved in planning an attack against the President.

Henry is told he only has two options. Option one is to reveal David's location to the authorities so the attack can be thwarted, but this would mean his son would face life in prison. Option two is to keep his son's location a secret, but the police are getting close to finding him and have "shoot to kill" instructions.

Surely, there must be a third option.

Book   (ISBN 978-1-7751699-1-8)
eBook (ISBN 978-1-7751699-2-5)

The Goliath Trilogy (Goliath, The Second Shooter, The Third Option) is also available as a single publication.

Book   (ISBN 978-1-7751699-3-2)
eBook (ISBN 978-1-7751699-4-9)

The Back Nine

Getting old is not for the squeamish. You have to deal with aging parents, kids who have moved out to make their own lives but who still need your help, and the realization that your lifelong career was just the halfway point. Your joints and muscles remind you that you can't do what the young guys do anymore. In addition, you discover that your relationship with your significant other has changed, but is now more important than ever.

This is a story about the members of the Riverview Golf Club as they face the challenges and joys of their golden years.

Welcome to the back nine – of your life.

Book   (ISBN 978-0-9921390-6-3)
eBook (ISBN 978-0-9921390-7-0)

The Legacy

Life is pretty good for the Baxter boys. Eric Baxter is a recent college graduate starting his career in financial planning. His younger brother, Chip, is a promising athlete heading off to compete at the Olympic Games in Brazil. And their father, Brian, has accumulated a tidy sum of money over his life.

As Eric prepares to start managing his father's money, he learns that his father's most important objective is to leave a legacy. But when Eric and his brother are kidnapped along with several other people while on a tour in Brazil, the legacy is in jeopardy.

Will the hostages be rescued before the final deadline is reached? Will Brian go against the recommendations of the FBI and the Brazilian police and pay the ransom? Their fate is determined in "The Legacy".

Book   (ISBN 978-0-9921390-2-5)
eBook (ISBN 978-0-9921390-3-2)

Choices

Jay Tremblay is an older man who heads off to a Las Vegas nightclub to attend the 50th anniversary of his university graduating class. "Choices" is the hottest new club on the strip because it has five separate clubs housed under the same roof, one featuring Pop music, one catering to Country & Western fans, another featuring Folk music, the fourth for those into the Blues, and the fifth club featuring music from the sixties. Jay soon discovers that this is not an ordinary nightclub because he starts having visions questioning all of the important choices he's made in his life. Should he have retired earlier? Should he have had children? Did he marry the right girl?

To make matters worse, the club is owned by Judy Prescott, an old girlfriend from his university days who he has been trying to avoid since graduation. This night could turn out to be one of the most important and revealing nights of his life.

eBook (ISBN 978-1-7751699-5-6)
AudioBook (ISBN 978-1-7751699-6-3)

Life-Changing Events

Sometimes an event happens that we know will affect us for the rest of our lives, whether we want it to or not. We might have been the perpetrator, or we might have been the victim, or maybe we're just the person in the wrong place at the wrong time.

Frank Taylor and Katy Sanchez share one of these life-changing events. It happened many years ago when Frank was a hard-working, middle-aged plumber and Katy was a troubled, eleven-year-old school girl. Both of them have been dealing with the fallout ever since.

They stumble across each other fifteen years later and Frank gets to see first-hand the impact his actions have had on Katy's life. He tries to help her get her life back on track without her finding out the role he played in turning her life upside down. But, is it too late, or will another life-changing event catch them both by surprise?

eBook (ISBN 978-1-7751699-7-0)

Choices & Life-Changing Events are also available together as a single publication.

Book   (ISBN 978-1-7751699-8-7)
eBook (ISBN 978-1-7751699-9-4)

The Journey

How do I get there from here? That's a question that we all face at some point in our lives.

The Journey is a story with four main characters, told through their own eyes, and each facing their own challenges. The year is 2038 and Ryan (the son) is an astronaut candidate with NASA, hoping to be one of the crew members selected for a future mission to Mars. There are numerous obstacles to overcome to make the six month journey there, achieve the goals of the mission, and then make the return trip back home to earth. Emma (the girlfriend) has her own goals in life and has to decide what she's willing to sacrifice to be with Ryan. Lori (Ryan's mother) has faith that her son will achieve his goals, but is facing her own challenging journey. Matt (Ryan's father) is an engineer who is coming to the realization that there are some things in life that he can't fully understand and fix, no matter how hard he tries, and sometimes you just have to have faith.

eBook (ISBN 978-1-7780648-1-4)
Paperback   (ISBN 978-1-7780648-0-7)
Hardcover (ISBN 978-1-7780648-2-1)

Women 101: A Father's Humorous Guide to his Son

Trevor McDonald is so hopeless with women that he has turned to his last resort for advice – his father. What could possibly go wrong? His father's first suggestion is that the Produce Department at the local grocery store is a good place to meet women and it goes downhill from there.

Will Trevor ever find the girl of his dreams? Read along as Dave gives his son advice on topics such as how to talk to women, compatibility, playing the field, and even sex. Plus, there's the lesson that seems to come up over and over again throughout his training – Women lie.

Book (ISBN 978-0-9921390-8-7)
eBook (ISBN 978-0-9921390-9-4)

Passenger 14C

When reporter Andrew McKenzie wakes up in Gander, Newfoundland, after an emergency landing of trans-Atlantic flight AC059, he discovers that he is one of the few people onboard the flight who is still alive. During the subsequent investigation by the authorities, he realizes he is no longer being treated as a lucky survivor, but has now become the prime suspect in a terrorist attack.

With the assistance of his nurse from the Intensive Care Unit, he is determined to find out what really happened onboard that flight and the role the mysterious passenger in seat 14C played in the tragedy.

Book   (ISBN 978-1-7780648-4-5)
eBook (ISBN 978-1-7780648-3-8)

Manufactured by Amazon.ca
Acheson, AB

12731245R00072